Dear Reader,

Did you ever have a girl pal who was smart and pretty, but so incredibly blind that she chased shallow studs who barely gave her the time of day? Oh, boy, I did. A few of them, actually. I'd bully and beg, but, oh no. She'd insist he was the one, and heartbreak here she comes. And meanwhile, there was this sweet guy who worshiped the ground she walked on.

Then I thought, hmm. What if she really did take my advice? Suppose—just as a matter of principle and a way to change her life for the better—a girl like my friend decided to ignore those bad boys in favor of the sweet but nondescript type? And then, what if, with all good intentions, she took it to extremes…?

And thus began Haley's search for the prince of frogs. This was, beyond anything I've ever written, the book of my heart. I hope you enjoy Rick and Haley's story as much as I did.

Wishing you romance and laughter,

Natalie Stenzel

"Haley, you've got to give Rick a chance."

She stared at her best friend as though Jen had suddenly grown a second head. "What are you saying? Have you forgotten my vow *not* to date princes? Rick is a total prince."

"I think you should reconsider. Your face lights up when you talk about him."

"Sure, he's hot. He's even fun to hang out with. But that's as far as I go. He's too good-looking."

Jen rolled her eyes.

"No, seriously, Jen, I'm through with good-looking men. I lose my head when they turn on the charm. And Rick is smooth. *Lethally* smooth."

"Maybe. I've only seen the guy once." Jen sounded entirely too doubtful for Haley's liking. "Hey, why don't you arrange for me to meet him again?"

"Forget it, Jen. There's no reason for you to check him out, because I'm not dating him. He's my neighbor and a *platonic* friend. End of story." And maybe if Haley repeated that often enough, she'd believe it, too.

Forget Prince Charming

Natalie Stenzel

TORONTO • NEW YORK • LONDON
AMSTERDAM • PARIS • SYDNEY • HAMBURG
STOCKHOLM • ATHENS • TOKYO • MILAN • MADRID
PRAGUE • WARSAW • BUDAPEST • AUCKLAND

If you purchased this book without a cover you should be aware
that this book is stolen property. It was reported as "unsold and
destroyed" to the publisher, and neither the author nor the
publisher has received any payment for this "stripped book."

This one's for Steve,
with all my love, for all the hours you
invested in my dream, and for believing in
me, long before I ever did.
You're one in a million.

ISBN 0-373-44178-9

FORGET PRINCE CHARMING

Copyright © 2003 by Natale Stenzel.

All rights reserved. Except for use in any review, the reproduction or
utilization of this work in whole or in part in any form by any electronic,
mechanical or other means, now known or hereafter invented, including
xerography, photocopying and recording, or in any information storage
or retrieval system, is forbidden without the written permission of the
publisher, Harlequin Enterprises Limited, 225 Duncan Mill Road,
Don Mills, Ontario, Canada M3B 3K9.

All characters in this book have no existence outside the imagination of
the author and have no relation whatsoever to anyone bearing the same
name or names. They are not even distantly inspired by any individual
known or unknown to the author, and all incidents are pure invention.

This edition published by arrangement with Harlequin Books S.A.

® and TM are trademarks of the publisher. Trademarks indicated with
® are registered in the United States Patent and Trademark Office, the
Canadian Trade Marks Office and in other countries.

Visit us at www.eHarlequin.com

Printed in U.S.A.

ABOUT THE AUTHOR

Natalie Stenzel was a girl who just couldn't keep her nose out of (gasp!) a romance novel. Still, she denied her dreamy inclinations long enough to earn respectable degrees in English literature and magazine journalism from the University of Missouri-Columbia. She even flirted with business writing and freelancing for a while, considered going back to school for another respectable degree...only to return to her one true love: romance. Born and raised in St. Louis, Missouri, Natalie now resides in lovely Virginia with her husband and two children, happy to live a dream (or several) come true.

Dear Reader,

When you're stressed out with the holidays and looking forward to stealing a little time for yourself, we've got the perfect solution! Pick up the latest Harlequin Flipside novel and take a well-deserved break. Our fun, witty and exciting romantic comedies will be sure to chase away the blues. Of course, if you're the type who loves the hustle and bustle, then the burst of energy you'll get from the book will make your day, too!

This month we're featuring *Do-Over* by Dorien Kelly. Have you ever *hidden* your true potential just to attract a guy? This heroine did it once, just once, and has regretted it ever since. She's always wanted to go back and do it differently. Looks as if she's getting her chance, because guess who's back in town....

We also have brand-new author Natalie Stenzel with *Forget Prince Charming*. Our heroine has discovered—the hard way—that those good-looking princes aren't always the best dates. So she's determined to find herself a "frog." But she can't catch any frogs if she can't see past her gorgeous neighbor!

These Harlequin Flipside books blend romance with a good dose of wit and cleverness and are sure to bring a smile to your face. Be sure to check us out online at www.harlequinflipside.com.

Enjoy!

Wanda Ottewell
Editor

Mary-Theresa Hussey
Executive Editor

1

"TO HELL WITH PRINCE CHARMING. I'll take the frog."

Haley Watson slammed into The Toy Boxx, sending the jingle bell above the door into a violent clanking. She tossed her purse under the sales counter and grabbed a broom. Soon she was swishing it back and forth with enough energy to send bits of straw flying in both directions.

Still muttering under her breath, Haley glanced over her shoulder to see Jennifer Grayson, her business partner, watching her. She'd been attending to a customer when Haley made her violent entry. Jen turned back to the tall man at her side, spoke a few words and gestured smilingly at a mountain of stuffed animals. Thus excusing herself, she approached Haley, giving the wildly swinging broom a wide berth.

"Trouble in fairy-tale land?" Jen murmured casually.

"You could say that." *Swipe, swish.*

Jen glanced at the blond man sorting through stuffed animals, then moved to discreetly block Haley from his view. "What happened?"

"Same old thing." *Swish, swish.* "You date a decent guy. He tells you he's in love." *Swish, slash.* "Then he ends up boffing his secretary behind your back anyway." She punctuated her words with a violent smack of the broom. *"Jerk."* At the last imprecation, their customer glanced back at them. Blue eyes studied them in open curiosity.

Smiling reassurance at the man, Jen plucked the broom from Haley's hands and set it aside. She led Haley by the elbow to a coloring table on the other side of the store.

"Sit."

Haley dropped into a child-size chair. The fit was perfect, as Haley wasn't much larger than a child herself. Her shoulders slumped and she twined her fingers together in a big, white-knuckled fist.

"Okay. Now give." Jen's voice was a soft command.

Haley blinked furiously at her tears, glancing at Jen and then away. "I wanted to surprise Peter. So I dropped by his office after lunch. I found him at his desk. With his secretary. And I don't think they were discussing business."

Jen's eyes widened. "Peter? Your boyfriend?"

"The guy who wanted me to spend the weekend on the lake with him? The guy who claims to love me? Yeah, that's the one. I walked in on them. Having sex on his desk."

Jen's lips tightened in sympathy. "Oh, Haley."

"He didn't even look up when I opened the door."

"He doesn't know you saw him with her?"

"Oh, he knows." Haley's voice grew stronger. "I got on his secretary's intercom and announced an emergency meeting in his office. ASAP. *That* got his attention."

"You didn't!"

"I did. And he all but shoved his new girlfriend off the desk trying to find his pants."

Jen tossed her head back, laughing. "Oh, that's good. I should have known you wouldn't just slink off quietly."

"Why should I?" Haley raised her chin, feeling militant on behalf of all womankind. Defiantly, she met the eyes of the blond man who was openly staring at them. He smiled slightly, disarmingly, then turned back to the mound of plush animals.

Jen, who missed the exchange, ended her laughter on a sigh. Her expression grew more serious as she studied her friend. "I'm glad you didn't let him get away with it." She paused then continued more softly. "Are you okay?"

Haley shrugged, the glow of victory fading to disappointment. "I'll live. At least I caught him before we went away together."

"Were you really going to spend the weekend with him?"

Haley shrugged. "I don't know. I hadn't really made up my mind yet. He seemed so perfect. He was handsome, charming, successful. He seemed to really care about me. Did I mention the handsome and charming part?"

Jen eyed her sympathetically. "It's rotten, I know. But I have to admit I'm kind of relieved. I was starting to worry that you were talking yourself into love with him just because everyone else thought he was wonderful."

Haley looked up in surprise. Jen had never voiced such doubts before. "I think I could have loved him. Or at least the man I thought he was." Her glance slid over to the blonde, who had dropped to one knee and was now studying a collection of trucks on a low shelf. Faded denim stretched taut across tight buttocks, the waistband gapping slightly in complement to the hard contours of the man's back. Annoyed with her wandering gaze, Haley forced her attention away from their customer. No more princes!

Jen tapped a long fingernail against her lips, her eyes narrowed thoughtfully. "I don't know. Has it occurred to you that you're not exactly heartbroken by what Peter did? Angry, sure. But devastated? No."

Haley weighed Jen's observation, honestly tried to picture herself living with Peter. Spending every day with him. She couldn't see it. How was that for honesty? "I guess Peter wasn't exactly the love of my life. It was humiliating to catch him cheating on me, though."

"Not as humiliating as having your co-workers catch you with your pants down, I'll bet."

At that, Haley managed to crack a tiny smile. "Good point."

Jen shook her head and squeezed Haley's shoulder. "You're better off without him."

"I know."

"You okay?"

Haley nodded and stood up.

"Good girl. I guess I'd better get back to it."

Jen retraced her way across the store. The blonde focused his smile on Jen, though his glance kept straying back to Haley.

Conscious of the tearstains on her face, Haley turned her back on the man. She picked up the broom she'd been abusing and resumed her task—without her earlier vigor. She pulled chairs out to sweep crayon bits off the floor, rearranged a stack of picture books and checked a dollhouse display for damage. She saw that only a tiny teacup had fallen prey to little fingers.

The Toy Boxx, located in a trendy little plaza in west St. Louis County, Missouri, was a popular hangout for kids whose parents were shopping at the nearby department store. Some of those faces had grown familiar and even dear to Haley over the summer. Now that school was in session, she'd miss the constant stream of pint-size customers. She loved their joy, their enthusiasm, even their mischief.

So when did such open, sincere creatures turn into the deceiving jerks she'd dated her whole life? she wondered.

Absently, she listened to Jen explaining the features of a remote control car. The deep rumble of a masculine voice echoed in the pit of her stomach. Haley forced herself not to look over her shoulder at the source.

Her dating failures had become so comical she and Jen had taken to nicknaming them. First there had been Football Flynn, her high school boyfriend who had played the field in more ways than one. Then there was her college sweetheart, dubbed Big-Man-On-Campus Brad. His charisma and wicked green eyes had charmed both her and her bank account into a puddle beneath his feet.

There had been a few casual relationships with men since then, but no one truly serious until Peter. He'd seemed so decent and so attractive, so incredibly perfect that she and Jen had dubbed him Prince Peter. That should have been her first clue. When he'd asked her out and intimated a future together, it had seemed almost too good to be true. She'd pictured herself living happily ever after with a handsome, loving husband. Some fairy tale this turned out to be. *Jerk.*

The unmistakable sound of the cash drawer opening and closing drew her attention.

"Thanks, Mr. Samuels. Have a nice day." The pleasant tones of Jen's voice were soothing to Haley.

"I appreciate the help." As he turned and strode toward the door, his eyes met Haley's. She stared. He smiled and nodded slightly before opening the door. The bell jingled cheerily after his exit. Something about the man seemed vaguely familiar. Haley frowned a moment, thoughtful, then shook her head and sighed. She couldn't place him.

She turned back to Jen. "Sorry I caused such a scene, especially with a customer in the store. It was incredibly unprofessional."

Jen grinned. "I don't think he minded." She hustled to the back room and returned with a box, which she passed off to Haley.

Haley set the box behind the cash register then began gathering up the defective toys to be returned. "I don't get it, Jen. Why do the men I date always turn out to be rotten? All men can't be that bad. Frank's not."

Jen smiled at the mention of her husband. "No, he's not."

"So how do I find *my* Frank?"

Jen paused thoughtfully. "I don't know. Patience helps. That way you're not rushing into relationships with men who aren't worth your time. Look around you. The nice guys aren't going to jump up and shout for attention. The attention hounds are probably the jerks you've been dating."

Haley considered that idea, thinking of the sexy blonde who'd just left the store. Much like Peter, the man had the kind of good looks and presence that commanded a woman's attention. "That makes sense, I suppose."

"Of course it does." Automatically smoothing a mailing label onto the box, Jen warmed up to her subject. "Women overlook the nice guys all the time. They don't even see the kind of guy who worships a girl in silence, who offers friendship but hopes for more. The guy who loses out. The nice guy who finishes last."

Enlightenment. Haley squeezed her eyes shut and groaned. "My mother was right. I should have married Jimmy Plankett."

"Jimmy who?"

"I'm an idiot. I can't believe I didn't realize all this before."

"Slow down, Haley. You're making my head spin."

"It's so simple. You're saying I've only been looking at the guys who attract lots of attention. The good-looking, charismatic ones. The kind of guy who can sweet-talk his way past a woman's good sense and straight into her heart." Haley started pacing furiously and gesturing with her hands as she worked through her developing theory.

"Right. So?"

"Well, a woman dazzled out of her common sense isn't going to pick up on all those little clues that should tell her the hunk has some major character flaws."

"Okay, I'm with you." She eyed Haley warily. "I think."

"Well, I'm tired of being dazzled and clueless. I'm tired of falling blindly for faithless jerks. It's too exhausting. I think it's time to take a more practical approach to finding a man. And this time I'm going to focus on a different breed of guy altogether."

Haley pressed a knuckle to pursed lips, realigning her thoughts before she continued in a thoughtful tone. "In order to find a guy like Frank or Jimmy, I really do need to ignore the good-looking Prince Charmings in this world. And start checking out the frogs."

"Uh-huh. You're losing me, Haley."

Haley sighed, wondering how to get her point across without being insulting. "I need to look for someone who isn't flashy or good-looking. When I'm with a hottie, I get all caught up in his looks and can't see past that. I want the nice guy who lost out to the gorgeous jerk. Basically, I need to find my very own sweet, reliable, but very overlookable—" She paused to look around, searching and sputtering, before settling almost defiantly on the appropriate term. "—*geek*."

Jen eyed her for a shocked moment. "I see. I don't know whether to be offended that you're calling Frank a geek or curious about this perfect Jimmy Plankett."

Haley waved her hands as if to erase the impression of her last statement. "I didn't mean anything personal against Frank. He's perfect. I want one just like him. All I meant in suggesting he was a geek is that you don't look at him the first time and immediately realize his great qualities. Nothing about him shouts Stud Muffin or Mr. Personality. But, according to you, he's a wonderful husband. Right?"

Jen laughed reluctantly. "Okay. I see what you're getting at. So tell me about Jimmy Plankett."

Haley paused, smiling slightly. "Jimmy Plankett gave me my first kiss."

"This makes him a geek?"

Haley turned stern eyes on her friend. "Do you want to hear this or not?"

"Sorry. You were saying?"

"Okay." Haley paused, gathering her thoughts. "I was in seventh grade and Jimmy and I had this mutual crush going on. We'd pass goopy notes and hold hands in the hallway. Innocent stuff." She closed her eyes, remembering. "He was very shy. Short, too. But nice eyes." She sighed. "Anyway. I could tell he wanted to kiss me for a long time but he couldn't quite work up the nerve. Then one day, right in front of my locker at school, he pulled me close and kissed me."

"How sweet." Jen smiled.

"Hmm. Yes. But then our braces locked together."

Jen groaned.

Haley nodded. "My algebra teacher had to walk us to the principal's office so they could call for help to untangle us. There we were, joined at the eyeteeth, stumbling down the hallway together with kids laughing and whispering. Talk about embarrassing." She grimaced momentarily then looked up to meet Jen's eyes. "But you know what? Jimmy held my hand through the whole thing."

"*He's* the perfect guy?"

Haley's smile was smug. "Even better. He's Mr. Sweet Geek, like your Frank. His kind of guy would never dream of cheating on his girlfriend."

"So, whatever happened to you two?"

This was the embarrassing part of the story. "Well, I kind of broke it off after the cutest guy in our class asked me to dance at the Spring Fling. I swear, for weeks and weeks after that I only had eyes for..." She paused, frowning. "You know, I can't even remember his name anymore. But I do remember Jimmy."

"Really." Jen gave her a pointed look.

Haley groaned. "Yes, *really*. Oh my God. That's my problem, isn't it? I never matured past the age of thirteen."

"Ah. Progress at last. So where do we find Jimmy Plankett?"

Haley made a face. "According to my mother, in Omaha, Nebraska, married with three kids. Mom keeps track of these things. Pulls them out with the guilt trips whenever she's interrogating me about my love life and her grandbaby prospects. The woman is dangerous, I tell you. Intelligent and subtly, persistently malicious."

Jen laughed. "She is not, you idiot. She just wants you to be happy and have lots of babies for her."

"Yes, I know, and if I don't find a man of my own, I guarantee she's going to find one for me."

"Why don't you let her? She probably meets available men every day at the TV station."

Haley gave her a harassed look. "Just whose side are you on anyway?"

Jen grinned back unrepentantly. "Yours, yours. Forgive me, I couldn't resist."

"I'll forgive you if you help me find a sweet geek of my own."

Jen's grin faded at the sincerity behind Haley's words. "You're serious about this." She stared hard at her friend and her voice grew cautious. "Now, Haley. I think you need to calm down a little before you do anything crazy. You've never been seriously attracted to a Frank or a Jimmy Plankett. I personally think you'd walk all over somebody like that. Besides that, don't you think you're tackling this project a little too soon after your breakup with Peter?"

Haley shook her head resolutely. "I'm twenty-eight, Jen, and the clock is ticking. Come on, you're only six months older than me and you already have a career, a husband, two kids and a mortgage. I'm way behind. And it's your duty, as my best friend and role model—"

"My duty!"

"—to help me catch up. So, where do I meet my man?" She looked up expectantly, never doubting that eventually...

Jen sighed, her gaze still on Haley. "Oh, all right. If you really want to do this, I'd better help you. With a plan as flaky as this, someone needs to keep an eye on you."

Seeing the doubt that still lingered on Jen's face, Haley sighed. "Look. I know all of this sounds hokey. Just another harebrained Haley scheme." She paused. "It's just that I've realized something about myself. Something bad enough to warrant drastic, corrective measures."

Jen gave her a curious look. "What?"

"Well...in all the ways that count, I guess I've been as much of an idiot about dating as these guys who keep disappointing me." Haley grimaced. "You don't fall in love with a guy's tight butt or cute grin. That's just stupid and shallow, but that's pretty much what I've been doing up to this point. So, in that respect at least, I suppose I've deserved every jerk I've ever dated.

"But I'm through with all that. I swear." Haley held up a hand as though vowing. "It's time I grew up and started looking a little deeper. And this plan..." She shrugged. "Well, look at it as a first step toward that."

Jen regarded her with new interest. "You know, Hale, I think that's the smartest thing you've said since you stormed into this place. Well, besides the part where you dumped Peter." She grinned.

"So that means you'll help me?"

"I said I would." Her eyes clouding in thought, Jen began taping up the box, winding, snipping and smoothing, her motions methodical.

"Thank God." Recognizing that Jen was now completely in her corner, Haley cased the front sidewalk for customers. No one in sight. She reached behind the counter for a clipboard and pen and looked up expectantly. "So where do we start?"

"Just hold on. I'm thinking."

Setting the clipboard on the counter, Haley wrote *Strategies for—* Then she paused, frowning. Something descriptive? Like *Finding my very own sweet and reliable, if*— Oh, just go for direct. *Strategies for Geek Hunting.* Good. To the point. She quickly scribbled it down and glanced up.

Her gaze directed out the front window, Jen was already muttering thoughtfully. "I guess the best way to approach this would be from a career and interest standpoint."

"Exactly. Career and interest. No shallow studs. I want a guy capable of conversation." She jotted *No studs.* "But how do I do that?"

"Hangouts, maybe?" Jen murmured doubtfully. "We could target a few interesting places and go from there."

"Right." Haley jotted *Target locations with high geek probability* and underlined it.

"Libraries, bookstores, computer stores. Hmm. That last one's good. You won't find some self-involved, directionless hunk in a computer store." Jen turned a speculative eye on her friend.

Haley was scribbling away furiously. "Computer store." She looked up. "Bingo. That's first. I'll try that new Computer Nation around the corner."

"Okay. But, Haley..."

"What?"

"Suppose you find a guy...like this. What will you do? How on earth are you going to approach him?"

"Well. Subtly, I suppose." Haley frowned. "I guess I need to adjust my attitude, huh? Take extra care choosing the guy...and then seem approachable?"

"Couldn't hurt."

"Right. Approachable. Maybe even tone down..."

"What?" Jen sounded alarmed.

"Just a sec." Haley, lost in thought, tapped her pen on the clipboard. She knew she tended to go overboard with her clothes sometimes. She hung out with kids and a friend most of the day, and bright colors were suitable for that. But this was different. She didn't want to scare guys away by dressing in neon colors or zebra stripes. She paused, then jotted *Dress down. Neutral classics. Nothing trendy.*

The guy could be shy, too. Shy guys would slip right past her usual radar unless... She scribbled some more. *Big smiles. Unthreatening but obvious approach.* Now, how to relax him so she could get to know him as he really was...maybe appeal to his strengths? Yes. *Stroke ego liberally.* She considered but refrained from underlining *liberally.* A girl had her limits.

Scanning her list and visualizing possibilities, Haley gave a decisive nod. "This could just work, Jen. And I think Computer Nation will make a perfect testing ground."

FLIPPING DOWN THE KICKSTAND of her bike, Haley propped it by her apartment door and turned to fiddle with the doorknob. She glanced distractedly at her new neighbor's door, and was surprised to find the hallway deserted for a change. Usually, she had to dodge several borderline hostile women, apparently lying in wait for her new neighbor, to get to her door. That was odd—and getting old. What sort of business was her neighbor in, anyway? It boggled the mind to wonder.

Grimacing, she gently worked at her key then turned the knob, but as usual, the lock refused to give. Haley grumbled and persisted, gritting her teeth and hoping her key wouldn't break off. "Come on you stubborn piece of—"

"Excuse me?"

Haley whipped around at the sound of a vaguely familiar voice, bumping her arm against the seat of her bike. The bike toppled, sending her purse and clipboard flying out of the basket attached to her handlebars. The clipboard caught the man in the shins. He winced.

Seeing his face contort, Haley grimaced herself. "Sorry. Are you okay?" After quickly righting her bike, she stepped forward, wanting to offer aid but not sure how to do it without touching the man's leg. Feeling a stranger's leg definitely overstepped a few boundaries.

The man looked up, a wary grin on his face.

Uh-oh. Oh, wow. The man had killer eyes. She stared into them. An incredible sapphire-blue. Not flat and cold like a stone, but deep and alive, almost liquid. She felt herself getting drawn in, feeling that pull of a too-good-looking-for-her-own-good man.

Then as she recognized the owner of those killer eyes, Haley froze. "You."

The amusement faded. "Me?"

"That's why you looked so familiar. You were at the store today and—"

"And I'm also your new neighbor. Right next door. Small world, huh?" He grinned uneasily.

From the look on his face, Haley could only surmise he wished it weren't quite this small. *Shake it off, Hale. The man's not for you and you're scaring him.*

She cleared her throat. "I— Hi. Look, I'm really sorry if that scene at the store today made you uncomfortable." She laughed. "The last thing I want to do is chase away new Toy Boxx customers." She shifted self-consciously. "Wow. You catch me freaking out on the job, arguing out loud with my door lock, and then I clobber you. I'm really sorry." Haley attempted a harmless neighbor grin. "Can I get you some ice for that?"

The man laughed, visibly relaxing. "I think I'll survive." He shifted the clipboard he'd retrieved from his shoes and tucked it under his arm. "I'm Ma—" He paused, coughing a little. "Sorry." He smiled and gestured apologetically. "Name's *Rick*. Rick Samuels." He offered his hand.

Haley took it, hoping her hand wasn't clammy with nerves and awakening hormones. "Haley Watson. Welcome to the building."

"It's good to finally meet my neighbor. I've been curious about you. The noises—"

Haley made a face. "My dog. Puppy actually. We're still working on housebreaking. Or rather, *I'm* working on it and Sherlock's trying his best to defeat me."

"So you're Watson and he's Sherlock?" Those blue eyes sparkled with amusement.

Haley grinned reluctantly. "I didn't name him. My ex-boyfriend did." She paused, her smile fading a little as she remembered the desk-bopping incident. "The dog used to be his."

"The detestable Prince Charming?"

Haley's regard cooled considerably. "You overheard."

He shrugged. "Not much. Just that it looked like you were pretty upset. I'm sorry things didn't work out."

He shifted awkwardly, as if at a loss for an appropriate response.

Haley relaxed. "Oh, it's okay, really. I've already had my revenge. I'm ready to move on now."

His eyes widened. "Your revenge?"

She waved a hand, smiling ruefully. "Don't ask. I had a psycho moment." A bark sounded from within, followed by a hopeful whine. Now, there was love and loyalty a girl could count on. Haley gazed at her closed door, smiling slightly as she pictured the puppy's sweet face.

"Revenge. Okay." Eyeing her with caution in between glances at her closed door, Rick started inching toward his own door.

Haley wondered at his reaction. Sure, she was babbling a bit, but— Her thoughts were distracted by the sight of her clipboard still tucked under his arm. Remembering the nature of the list on the front page, she gasped and lurched forward, arm outstretched.

Rick's eyes widened at the sudden movement. Yanking open his door, he swiftly ducked inside.

"Wait! You've got my—" the door slammed "—clipboard." Her words ended on a note of dread. Leaning her forehead against his door, she stabbed repeatedly at the doorbell. Silence. Great. Now her hunky new neighbour would know all about her plans to catch herself a frog.

Inside, Rick stared at the closed door, his thoughts a contradictory jumble. He couldn't decide whether he'd just experienced a narrow escape or an intriguing first encounter with his sexy neighbor. Earlier today, she'd stormed her way into the toy shop like a woman bent on violence. Now, he was left to wonder if filing a custody suit for a dog—or even all-out stealing the poor beast—was her idea of revenge. Talk about malicious.

And disillusioning. He'd caught sight of his new neighbor the day he'd moved into the building. Ever since then, he'd found himself anticipating the occasional glimpse of her. All that bustling energy, the lightning-flash smiles and expressive eyes. She was fascinating to watch. And he really had a weakness for freckled noses.

When the landlady mentioned this morning that Haley worked at The Toy Boxx, very near where he worked himself, he'd decided to shop there for a birthday gift for his nephew. Part owner of a toy shop, he'd decided, was a perfect occupation for Haley.

Too bad she was turning out to be such a head case. A smart man would be resisting the temptation, he knew. At least for right now. The town's population of single females had wigged out on him since a gossipy local celebrity listed him as one of the most eligible bachelors in the metro area.

Now, the scent of money was attracting desperate women faster than he could shoo them off. They didn't seem to care who he was or what he was about, just that he had a bank account that could support extravagant shopping sprees. For all he knew, this Haley was just another woman anxious to get her hands on a fat wallet.

Shrugging philosophically, he reached over and flipped on the stereo to a classic rock station and cranked it up, letting the throbbing rhythm work the kinks out of his shoulders. That's when he noticed the clipboard still tucked under his arm. He pulled it out, intending to discreetly return it to his crazy neighbor, when the title, scrawled in red ink and underlined, caught his attention. Strategies for Geek Hunting.

2

Strategies for Geek Hunting?

"What the...?" He read further down the page, unable to help himself. He couldn't prevent either the disbelieving grin that spread across his face or the old defensiveness that stiffened his spine. Automatically he reached up with an index finger to the bridge of his nose but found nothing there.

...Targeting...high geek probability...

He dropped his hand to his side, his defensiveness hardening into resolve. The woman was looney tunes and some poor, unsuspecting Joe out there—

...stroke ego liberally...

He shook his head. Oh, no. Not on his watch. And watch her he would. If he happened to enjoy the view just a little too much, well, that was too damn bad. Sure, she was a sexy woman, but a man had to have standards. He skimmed and reskimmed the page, his scowl deepening with every outrageous word.

Feeling the need to vent on the person who drew up this crazy, demoralizing plan, Rick stalked to the door, swung it open...and promptly caught Haley in his arms.

Frustrated and embarrassed, Haley glared at him as he set her back on her feet. Encountering the less than friendly look in his eyes, she tempered her own hostility and retreated a pace. "Don't you answer your door?" She shoved her hair behind her ears.

"My door? Oh, the doorbell doesn't work. You should have knocked."

"I did." She gritted the words out.

"Hmm. Well, I did have the stereo cranked up."

"Whatever. Can I please just have my clipboard back?"

Rick smiled down at her, his expression as innocent as a child's. "So you're going hunting?"

Haley made a desperate grab for the clipboard but he casually held it just out of reach. Her panic congealed into embarrassed frustration. "You just had to read it, didn't you. Brand new to the building, and you're already pulling the nosy neighbor act."

"Hey, you're the one who clobbered me with a clipboard. All I did was pick it up. Never mind that, though. Tell me about the hunt. Is it some twisted cultural supremacy thing? Down with geeks, dweebs and nerds?"

Haley studied him momentarily. Thinking. Maybe he hadn't read the whole thing. Maybe he'd just glanced at the title. Sighting an out, she attempted a breezy smile. "It was just a joke. Like those 'you know you're a redneck when' kind that are everywhere now."

Rick's smile hardened but he let her snag the clipboard out of his hands. "Looked like a pretty involved joke. Kind of a humorous how-to manual, I suppose? So, once you hunt up one of those suckers, what are you supposed to do with him? Reform him or just enjoy him as he is?"

She hugged the clipboard to her chest, heart pounding with new unease. "Um. I'm not sure. A friend just, well, a friend of mine scribbled it down for me. We had customers and she didn't want to offend anyone, so she just wrote it down for me to read later. And I will. With dinner probably." Haley wished she could spontaneously combust. Now. If she would only learn when to shut up, maybe she could pull off a believable lie.

"Oh, sure." He nodded agreeably. "I always enjoy a good joke with my dinner. Hell, to hear a good joke, I'd be willing to buy you dinner." An unholy gleam in his eyes, Rick leaned one shoulder against the doorjamb, folded his arms and grinned down at her. He was obviously aware of her silent squirming and enjoying it immensely. "So how about it? Dinner for a joke?"

Haley glared at him. "You read the whole thing."

"Okay, I skimmed it. You caught me. That's not to say I don't have a million questions, though. You could tell me all about it over dinner. What do you say? My offer still stands."

Haley squeezed her eyes shut, but she could still picture his wicked grin. Naturally, the grin—what was she thinking? *the whole package surrounding the grin*— was so attractive she could just die. She was destined to forever be humiliated in front of sexy men. And be attracted to them anyway, masochistic idiot that she was.

With the battle of the senses raging within her, Haley couldn't help but wonder if it was a blessing or a curse that she'd sworn off hunks. Because, despite his provoking manner, Rick Samuels fairly defined the term. It was no wonder he had women lining up outside his door. Twelve short months ago—hell, twelve short hours ago—she'd have been tempted to do the same. The man was hot.

He looked to be in his early thirties, with Brad Pitt's good looks, only taller, with broader shoulders and more rugged features. And she was pretty sure the sun-kissed color of this guy's hair was real. Thick and unruly, ending just about collar-level. She sighed. And those deep blue eyes and wicked lips set a girl to dreaming of laughter and hot sex. God help her. She opened her eyes slowly, trying to brace herself.

He was still watching her, no doubt savoring the embarrassment behind her hesitation. "Well, Haley? Care to get to know your neighbor?"

Oh, boy would I! "No, thank you. I have a lot to do tonight."

"Too bad." His grin didn't falter. "Some other time, maybe?" At her reluctant nod, he straightened and strode past her into the hallway toward her bike. "Just let me wheel this in for you and I'll get out of your way so you can get started on your project."

In the interest of ending the humiliating encounter, Haley bit back a choice insult and turned to continue wrestling with her door. Naturally, the key turned smoothly this time. The door all but sprung open in her hands. She set her clipboard on a lamp table then stood back to let Rick push her bike into the living room.

Sherlock's frantic barking echoed from the back of the apartment. Haley sighed. It sounded like the dog had managed to shut himself in the closet again. She wondered how many shoes had been sacrificed today.

"The boyfriend's dog?" Rick's eyes were trained on

the doorless opening to her loft bedroom. She thought she could see suspicion and disapproval in his eyes.

"My dog, now."

His eyes narrowed. "Yes, so you said. Some revenge."

Haley frowned. "Huh?"

"Stealing a man's best friend from him."

Haley's jaw dropped. "I didn't *steal* him. Peter abandoned the poor thing. Almost."

"Right." His voice rang with doubt.

She propped her fists on her hips. "I'm not lying. He passed the dog off to me. Weeks ago. He said he traveled too much to take care of it and the dog liked me better anyway." She shrugged uncomfortably. "And I didn't have the heart to take him to the humane society or find a stranger to take him in. So the puppy's mine." She glared at Rick. "Do you always jump to wild conclusions?"

He had the grace to look embarrassed. "I hope not. Sorry."

Haley rolled her eyes. "Like I'd kidnap somebody's dog."

Rick cleared his throat and glanced around the apartment before turning his sights back on the bike. His eyes flickered over the banana seat and woven basket decorated with plastic daisies. The bicycle only had one speed. It was similar, in fact, to the bike she'd ridden all over the neighborhood as a child. He swept a hand over the upright handlebars, fitting his fingers around the tasseled grips, then looked up to meet her eyes with a provoking grin. "Nice bike."

Haley sighed, used to the odd looks and comments

she attracted with her metallic-blue 1976 Huffy. "It does the job and it's made for a short person." She paused a beat. "And I already killed two ten-speeds because I never remembered to shift gears properly. This was ten bucks at a garage sale and it's perfect for the short trip to work. Saves on gas."

Casually, he tested the front tire, a slight frown wrinkling his brow. "You need new tires. These are almost bald. Why don't you come by my shop this weekend and I'll get you set up." His offer was absently sincere and, from the look on his face, almost immediately regretted.

"You own a bike shop?"

"Mmm. The one around the corner from your toy shop."

She eyed his physique, which obviously carried not one extra pound of fat, and conceded that he was very likely a biking enthusiast. Peter had been, too. In between tennis matches, he'd participated in a triathlon last year, a fact he liked to work into conversations with new acquaintances. And complete strangers. She gave Rick a cool smile. "I suppose you race, too."

"Sometimes. Just a hobby." He looked as though he were going to add something to that statement, then shrugged and smiled.

"Well, maybe I'll have those tires looked at sometime. Thanks."

"No problem. Guess I'd better leave you to it." He nodded meaningfully at the clipboard, his eyes sparkling wickedly.

Her annoyance grew. "Yes, I suppose you'd better. Nice meeting you, Rick."

"You, too, Haley. Incidentally, you might also try copy centers and, maybe, hobby shops." He closed the door behind him, and Haley stuck her tongue out at it. Maybe not the most mature response, but it was gratifying.

A moment later, she snatched up her clipboard again and added these two items to her list of likely hangouts.

HER HAIR DRIPPING WET, Haley considered the options overflowing her closet. The packaging could make or break her, she knew. Best to go with something simple. Attractive but not threatening.

She tugged the fluffy towel more firmly around her breasts. With her free hand, she shoved aside bright colors, short hems and trendy cuts, before pulling out a pair of mostly unwrinkled khaki pants. What about tops? A simple long-sleeved T-shirt maybe? She tossed her finds into a pile on the bed and dropped the towel.

Opening a drawer of the antique dresser she'd refinished herself, she pulled out a pair of lacy peach panties and matching bra and pulled them on. Then she shrugged into her T-shirt and hopped her way into her slacks. After buckling the woven leather belt, she surveyed the effect in the mirror. Acceptable. Impatiently she flipped a wet lock of hair out of her face and behind an ear.

Earrings. Jewelry. What about jewelry? Simple hoop earrings. And her locket. Haley tapped a finger to her mouth. That would be perfect. A simple gold heart on a dainty chain, a Valentine's Day gift from her late father. For luck.

She glanced wistfully at the chunky bangles she'd picked up at a flea market to go with a skinny little dress she'd found on sale a few months ago. Shaking her head resolutely, Haley closed her jewelry box. She went scavenging for a matched pair of socks, slipped them on, and reached for a hairbrush.

After ten minutes' worth of blow-drying her reddish-brown hair and applying a touch of makeup, Haley decided she was as ready as she'd ever be. She ran down the stairs from her loft bedroom, grabbed her purse and headed out the door.

Thirty seconds later, she turned back and unlocked the door. She dug through a drawer of her desk until she found her computer manual, then hurried out once more.

She was dressed and armed.

"WELCOME TO COMPUTER NATION, ma'am. Is there something I can help you find?"

Haley turned in the direction of that nervous voice and came face to face with her first real-live computer nerd. Cruel to say it, even think it, she knew, but he certainly fit every stereotype she'd ever heard.

His brown eyes eager behind thick lenses, the man smiled at her, shifting nervously from one thin leg to the other. Kind of endearing, she allowed doubtfully. Certainly sincere. Haley's smile widened. "I certainly hope so...Tim," she finished, after reading the badge pinned to his ink-stained shirt.

Tim flushed, but he clapped his hands together gamely. "Okay, where do we start?"

"Well, I'm looking for a good financial management

system. Computerized, obviously. Something to help me keep track of my accounts, maybe set up a budget." Haley carefully injected a delicate air of helplessness into her request. She wasn't lying about her need for software, but she probably could have selected it without any help.

Her delivery must have worked, too, because Tim was looking a little more at ease, obviously in his element now. "I think we can help you out. We have a pretty good selection, appropriate for different computers, different needs. Some of them are loaded onto the demo computers if you want to try them out."

"Oh, good. I really think I'm going to need to try them all out before I know which one is right for me."

At her dazzling smile, Tim flushed.

The man poised around the corner of an aisle, who'd turned at the sound of the familiar voice, rolled his eyes in disbelief. *This was going to be good.*

Keeping his distance, Rick kept pace with them, making sure to keep an aisle or display as buffer between him and the conversing couple.

Unable to resist a quick glance at his attractive neighbor, Rick peeked around the corner, chuckling silently at the wide-eyed look she was giving poor Tim. No doubt Tim was ready to spontaneously combust. The look was obviously meant to boost a fragile male ego, and it was working. In spades.

When Tim moved closer to demonstrate with the mouse while Haley stood at the keyboard, Rick's amusement faded. Haley didn't back away, and his mood lowered even more.

"Oh, Tim, that's perfect. I've had so much trouble

keeping track of my spending from month to month, but I think this program would keep even me on track. Do you think it will work with any computer?"

Tim's voice and posture grew even more confident as he discussed computer speed, memory and various other factors that were only so much white noise to Rick. He'd already determined the maker and capabilities of the software Tim had demonstrated and knew it was compatible with almost any system. Tim did, too, he was sure, and was now just trying to impress the lady with his prowess.

To his disgust, Haley was wearing the most vacuously fascinated expression he'd ever seen on an intelligent woman's face. Unable to bear witness to any more, Rick quickly selected an ink cartridge to fit the printer in his home office and headed toward the checkout lines.

He smiled at the cashier. "Hi, Cathy. Doing all right up here?"

"Yes, Mr. Samuels. I think I'm going to like working here." She smiled at him.

"Good, good. If you have any questions, just ask Tim. He's in charge of the store while I'm gone. I'll see you in the morning." He frowned. "No, wait. I'm putting time in at the bike shop tomorrow. Pass that along to Tim for me, would you? I'll be back the day after, but he can call me if he runs into any problems."

"Sure thing, Boss."

As he was turning to leave, Rick heard the sound of Haley's voice from somewhere close behind him.

"...Thank you so much for all your help, Tim. I'm

pretty clueless when it comes to the nuts and bolts of computers."

"My pleasure."

Haley's voice lowered. "I'll see you Friday, then."

Rick glanced over his shoulder, truly peeved now. Despite his unquestionable intelligence, Tim was grinning like a fool, patting his pocket and verbally tripping over himself in his effort to please.

"...I have your number right here. I'll call you after I'm off work for directions."

When Tim turned with obvious reluctance to greet a new customer, Haley went to pay for her new software, a satisfied smile on her face.

Still unaccountably annoyed, Rick exited the store, intending to lie in wait for her. He'd force himself to forget the sight of Haley playing up to Tim and instead play the cool, sophisticated interrogator so he could determine Haley's intentions.

After all, Tim was young and impressionable. He deserved better than to be hurt by Haley's geek-hunting ways. As Tim's boss and friend, and knowing what he knew about Haley, Rick felt responsible for the guy. He was just doing Tim a good turn. Yeah, that's the way he'd play it. Nothing personal; he was just looking out for his fellow man.

And he damn well was *not* going to act like a jealous, lovesick puppy. Even if he felt like one.

"EXPENSIVE FIRST DATE, Haley?" The male voice came from just over her right shoulder as Haley stepped out into the sunlight.

Her heart dropping to her knees, Haley whirled to

face her provoking new neighbor. "Don't you know better than to sneak up behind unsuspecting women?"

"Sorry. Didn't mean to scare you."

"What are you doing here anyway?" She turned and walked toward her car.

"I was just picking up some ink for my printer." Rick shrugged and fell easily into step with her, his long legs taking one step for every two of hers. "I happened to hear a familiar voice and listened in. Boy, were you laying it on thick in there."

"Just what are you trying to suggest?"

"I'm not suggesting anything. I've read that list of yours and I saw you moving in for the kill back there. It worked, too. Poor sucker didn't even know what hit him, did he?" Rick shook his head in mock sorrow.

"You don't know what you're talking about."

"Oh, I think so. You went into that computer store intending to pick up some poor schmuck. You found him, buttered him up, and he was yours for the taking."

Haley gritted her teeth but spoke evenly. "I went into that computer store to buy software. Tim was kind enough to help me and we had an enjoyable conversation. He asked me out Friday. I accepted. Simple as that."

"Wow. A whole week in advance? Guy must be desperate."

Haley's jaw flexed harder, but she managed to hold on to the worst of her temper. "What is it with you? Is all of this because of what you read on my clipboard? Look, I apologize if you were offended, but it wasn't meant to be seen by anyone but me. So why don't you just put it out of your mind and we'll both feel so much better.'' She turned and marched off.

Rick hurried after her, catching her elbow before she could unlock her car door.

Haley froze, trying to ignore all the nerve endings that sprang to life at his touch. *Not interested in princes. Not interested in princes.* Maybe if she repeated that often enough it would be true.

He gentled his grip but didn't release her. ''Look, I'm sorry, okay? I guess it was just hard to have you turn me down flat yesterday then watch you make a date with another guy today. But I can take no for an answer.'' He smiled ruefully, his eyes boyishly charming. ''We're neighbors. It's probably not a good idea to go to war, right?''

Nervously, Haley began weaving her key chain in and out of her fingers, the tinkling sound helping to distract her from his nearness. She nodded. ''Okay. Let's just call a truce. Fair enough?'' She glanced up cautiously.

Rick was shaking his head, his blue eyes reflecting the cool shade of the cloudless sky. ''Nope. Not good enough. Let's start over. Hi. My name's Rick. You must be Haley, my next-door neighbor. How do you do?'' He lifted the arm he still grasped and held its hand with his free one in a firm, if puppetlike, handshake.

Haley rolled her eyes at his clowning attempt but weakened under the pressure of that contagious smile. She sighed and reluctantly smiled back at him. ''Hi, Rick. Nice to meet you. I hope my dog Sherlock hasn't been disturbing you with all his barking.''

"I like dogs. You should introduce us some time. Like tonight maybe? Care to have me over for pizza?"

Her eyes narrowed. "I thought you could take no for an answer."

"Come on, just pizza between neighbors. I promise. My treat. You can fill me in on the building. You know, good gossip, dos and don'ts, how to get on the manager's good side so I can get my doorbell fixed. Harmless stuff."

She eyed him warily, remembering the sourpuss who used to live in the next-door apartment. The older woman hadn't been as understanding about Sherlock's barking. Haley had been anticipating an eviction notice when the woman finally moved out. Given the unexpected reprieve, it behooved her to get along with her new neighbor if at all possible. "Well, as long as you're not some serial killer or anything—"

"Nope. I'm harmless. Mostly. Besides, you have Sherlock for protection. He can chaperon."

Haley nodded slowly. Belatedly, she realized her hand was still in his and she pulled it free of his warmth. "I suppose that would be all right. We're neighbors. It only makes sense to get acquainted."

"That's the spirit. So, what time's good for you?"

Haley looked at her watch. "Well, I need to stop off at the shop, see how things went today. So, how about giving me about an hour and a half, maybe two hours?"

"So, around five-thirty or six? Your place? I'll bring pizza and napkins."

"Make it six and you've got yourself a—"

"—date?" Rick's eyes widened with sparkling innocence.

"—*deal*." Haley eyed him doubtfully. "This is not a date. We're just neighbors getting acquainted."

"Okay, if you say so. See you at six, Haley."

Twenty minutes later, Haley swung into The Toy Boxx and flipped the sign to Closed. It was ten minutes early, but the shop was empty and she needed to debrief in private. She patted her pockets, dug through her purse. Key...in her desk. She'd lock up later.

"I'll be with you in a minute." Jen's voice drifted pleasantly from the back room.

"Take your time. It's just me. And I closed the shop." Haley tossed her purse on the counter and turned to pull down the blinds.

"So what happened?" Jen emerged from the back room, carrying a box of shopping bags with the store's logo on the front. She stashed them under the counter and pulled out an old-fashioned feather duster.

"I've got a date. Two, kind of, if you count Rick."

Jen's eyes widened. "Tell me."

Haley started tidying shelves, straightening fallen teddy bears and restacking packaged cars. As she did so, she described her encounter with Tim.

"Okay, so what did you think of him?" Jen asked when Haley wound down.

Haley shrugged. "He seemed like a nice guy."

"Did you discuss anything besides financial software?" Jen asked, mildly exasperated.

"Well, my computer, the system here." Haley smoothed the hair on a doll before setting her next to her sisters. She looked up. "What more do you want? I only spoke to him for about twenty minutes and I was there for software. He seemed nice, he asked me out, and I decided, 'Why not?'"

Jen shook her head and began whisking the duster back and forth across the blinds.

Noticing the head shaking and the rueful smile on her friend's face, Haley threw out her hands in disgust. "What? I met what appeared to be a nice, unassuming kind of guy. A geek, if you want to be unkind about it. And he asked me out. Mission accomplished, right?"

"I knew this was a mistake, Haley. At this rate, you're going to end up either stuck with some reliable guy who means nothing to you, or still dating at the age of ninety."

Haley laughed. "I don't think I'm that hopeless. I just need to get my feet wet, you know? I haven't dated anyone but the prince charmings of the world. If things work out with Tim, great. If not, no harm done. Consider it a practice date."

Jen studied her friend. "I suppose that's reasonable." She smiled slightly, her eyes narrowing. "So tell me about this Rick."

"Well, you've already met him. He was the guy who was in here the other day while I was having my tantrum."

Jen's eyes widened and she smiled. "Oooh, Haley. Very nice."

Haley made a face. "He's also my new neighbor."

"Your *neighbor*?"

"Next door. He's coming over tonight for pizza." Haley regarded Jen sternly. "But it's just a neighbor thing."

"Why?" Jen eyed her as if Haley had lost her mind.

Haley plopped down on the floor. She rested back against a massive teddy bear, letting its huge arms encircle her shoulders. "Because he's beautiful. Mouthwatering."

Jen stopped dusting. "And?"

"What else is there to say? He's a hunk and I've sworn off hunks." At that reminder, Haley dropped her hot face into her hands. "And he knows it." The last came out in an embarrassed squeak.

"He knows it? What did you do? Tell him?" Jen's voice rose in disbelief.

Haley looked up, her cheeks still hot. "Of course not. I'm not that stupid." She described their encounter in the hallway, ending with a disgruntled sigh. "So, I guess that will teach me not to put incriminating evidence in writing."

"Oh, Haley." Jen grimaced in sympathy. "So, how did all this evolve into a pizza date tonight?"

"Well, I ran into him at the computer store today." Haley whipped her hair behind her ears, the movement vicious. "He heard me with Tim. I must have sounded like a complete idiot. Defenseless maiden in need of guidance from the computer expert." When Jen rolled her eyes, Haley's voice rose in her own defense. "Tim was nervous of me. I had to do something to put him at ease. What would you have done?"

Jen shrugged. "So how did Rick react to all this?"

"He seemed kind of put off by it."

"And that's why you're having dinner together tonight?" Jen sounded baffled.

"I guess he decided to give me the benefit of the doubt. In the interest of good neighbor relations."

Jen smiled shrewdly at her friend. "Pretty lame, but I'll buy it if you want me to. Tell me about Rick. Does he have anything approaching a personality? What about a job?"

Haley sighed in frustration but calmed enough to consider the questions. "Well, you know he's good-looking. Kind of like Brad Pitt, but bigger, less pretty. Remember? And these incredible blue eyes." She smiled ruefully. "Plus a body that won't quit. Nice shoulders, tall, he obviously works out. I know he bikes. In fact, he owns a bike shop. As far as personality goes, though," Haley frowned, irritation darkening her eyes, "he's just what you'd expect from a guy who looks like that."

"Boring?"

One eyebrow rose. "No, that he's not. Just arrogant and provoking. Endlessly, annoyingly provoking. It's like sparring with an immature older brother."

Jen burst out laughing. "He sounds perfect for you. Have your pizza and your man with my blessings."

"Now wait just a minute—"

A jingle and an imperious voice interrupted her protest. "Hello? Darling?"

Haley jumped to her feet. "Mom!"

She watched in mingled delight and dread as her smartly dressed mother strode crisply into the store. She tugged Haley into her arms for a warm hug.

Haley returned the hug absently, her eyes taking in the sight of the man who had sauntered in behind her. Oh, boy. Not again. Damn, she should have locked the door. Not that she minded the view. Indeed, it was fine. Too fine. Her mother was trying to stack the deck against her.

She pulled back, smiling determinedly at her mother. "What brings you here today?" *As if I didn't know.*

Clara Watson just as determinedly ignored the silent accusation. "I wanted to visit my daughter and I brought along a friend." She turned a brilliant smile on Mr. Smooth, Dark and Sculpted. "Adam Harding, I'd like you to meet my daughter, Haley."

Haley transferred her gaze to the man who appeared to be in his mid-thirties. He was undeniably good-looking, a few inches shy of six feet tall, and wearing a smile that radiated charisma. Haley offered her hand and a polite smile. "Hello, Adam. Nice to meet you." She withdrew her hand after a brief shake. "So how do you two know each other?"

Clara smiled proudly. "We featured Adam on the Show Me Show a few weeks ago, and I have to say he looked just marvelous on TV. The camera adores him. My ratings went right through the roof that morning. He also happens to be local, can you believe it?" She gazed meaningfully at her daughter. "In fact, his family's been local for over a hundred years. Isn't that right, Adam?"

"Yes, ma'am." It was a rich, smooth voice, but somehow it fell flat on Haley's ears. Maybe she was actually building up a resistance to gorgeous, charming men. "You have a beautiful mother and an intriguing store, Haley. It's nice to meet you."

"Thank you." Haley's smile felt tight. She felt her

mother's unspoken command to turn on the sparkling wit and ignored it, remaining stubbornly nonsparkling. She felt Jen move up beside her, silently amused but supportive.

"Hi, Mrs. Watson." She greeted Clara then turned to the man at her side. "Hi, I'm Jennifer Grayson, Haley's business partner." She offered her hand.

"Oh, good. Perhaps you could help me find a book for my niece while Haley and Clara visit?" He smiled charmingly as he shook hands.

Jen's smile was dazzling. Haley resisted the urge to stomp on her friend's foot. Her mother didn't need *any* encouragement—and Jen was happily married.

Jen tossed her a glance, easily interpreted as *I'm married, not dead.* Then she gestured to the books across the store as she led the way, chatting politely with Adam.

Haley turned back to her mother.

"Isn't he handsome?" Clara's hushed voice vibrated with enthusiasm.

"Oh, very."

"He's rich, too. All kinds of attorneys and judges and business people in his family. An established name, good connections. And so charming. He took me to lunch the other day and ordered in French. Very impressive. Don't you think so?" Her sparkling eyes avidly perused the tall man.

"Oh, sure." Haley's eyes remained stubbornly on her mother.

At Haley's flat tone, Clara turned back to frown at her daughter. "So why am I getting this attitude? I worked very hard to find a man I thought would impress you."

Haley gritted her teeth. "I appreciate all the hard work, Mom, but please stop all this. It's humiliating. Do you think I'm so unattractive I can't find a man myself?"

"Oh, no, honey. I'm just trying to save time. At twenty-eight, your childbearing years are slipping away before my eyes. I want grandchildren before I'm old and drooling in the home."

"Mom!"

"Honestly, Haley. Your father's gone, and you're all I have left. It would break my heart if you didn't start a family of your own. I don't want you to be lonely, and frankly, I don't want to die alone while you work yourself to death."

"If you're so lonely, maybe you ought to be the one dating, not me." As soon as the words left her mouth, Haley wished she could call them back. She stared into her mother's wide eyes. "Oh, Mom. I'm sorry. Really. I know you and Daddy—I didn't mean—"

Clara stared, her perfectly powdered chin quivering slightly. "No, it's okay. Maybe you're right. Maybe I've been putting too much of a burden on your shoulders. I'm sorry." She made a visible effort to smile. "I guess I won't call the other men on the list, then."

"List?"

Clara waved it off. "Never mind."

A *cha-ching* of the cash register distracted them both, and soon Jen and Adam joined them. After a few moments of polite conversation, during which Haley felt lower and lower, Clara and Adam left together.

After the door closed behind them, Haley slumped into a miniature chair. "I'm pond scum. Absolute slime. Lower than slime. Bacteria reject me as substandard host material." Haltingly, Haley related events to Jen. "And Dad's only been gone three years. Mom was devastated. I'm such a creep."

Jen shook her head, a sympathetic smile on her face. "That was a little rough, Haley."

"No kidding. I'm really tired of her parading men in front of me, but I could have just said so without being mean."

Jen cocked her head. "Oh, I don't know. Maybe she needed to hear the 'mean' part, too. Your mom's an attractive woman still."

Haley's eyebrows raised high. "You think she should start dating again? But she's my *mother*."

"Oh, don't be juvenile, Haley." Jen spoke with the blunt familiarity of lifelong friendship. When you shared jump rope, puberty and boys, then remained friends into adulthood, there wasn't much you couldn't say to one another.

Haley sighed. "I suppose. I'm still going to call her and apologize, though."

"Mmm. Not a bad idea. Sure you don't want to date Adam?"

"I'm sure."

Jen smiled. "Something tells me you prefer tall blond men who like dogs, bikes and pizza. Right?"

"Wrong."

"Oh, come on. He sounds fantastic. I think you should go out with him."

Haley eyed her incredulously. "Hello? Where were you when we talked about all this earlier? I'm through with the Adams and the Ricks of this world. Not only is

Rick a hunk, just like all the other jerks I've dated, but he also annoys me to no end. Do you want to see me arrested for murder? Some friend you are."

"I'm sure you're right." But Jen still looked highly amused.

Haley scowled and finished reorganizing the boxed games before helping Jen lock up for the rest of the weekend. No way would she admit that she still couldn't rid her memory of a pair of wicked blue eyes taunting and tempting her. She headed home with not a few misgivings about the evening's plans.

3

WHEN THE DOORBELL RANG promptly at six, Haley wiped nervous palms on her jeans. The pants were part of the third outfit she'd tried on this evening. She'd wanted to strike just the right note of casual friendliness. This was *not* a date.

Still, she couldn't set her vanity aside so completely as to dress in her scrubbiest clothes. She'd finally settled on worn but figure-hugging jeans, and a pretty V-neck T-shirt in a shade of coral that did nice things for her hair and complexion. Attractive without being provocative. Okay. She was ready.

Plastering a friendly smile on her face, Haley swung the door open. And forgot to breathe.

There Rick stood, sinfully masculine in faded jeans and a white T-shirt. Granted, the outfit was simple, but when those clothes, simple as they were, were wrapped around a body like Rick's, they took on a life and sexuality of their own.

"Hi." Rick stood grinning in the doorway, a pizza box in his hands. His grin faltered at her lack of response. "All right if I come in?"

Haley jumped. Inhaled. "Oh, sure." She stepped back—way back—to admit him. One touch, and dear lord, she'd—

"Great. I brought a six-pack, too. Do you drink beer?" He sent a curious glance over his shoulder.

"Oh, sure." *Do you drink arsenic, Haley? Oh, sure, Rick, anything you offer me with that sexy wave of hair falling over your eye...getting all tangled up with long, silky eyelashes. Oh, heaven help me.*

"So where's our chaperon?" Rick set the pizza down on the table and looked around the apartment, his gaze traveling up the stairs. At the top was a tall, well-chewed baby gate Haley had fashioned in front of the entrance to her loft bedroom. A dark-eyed puppy with floppy ears and massive paws stared down at him. The dog, a chocolate Labrador, whined pathetically from behind the barrier. Rick grinned and turned back to Haley.

"Sherlock?"

"The dog I kidnapped, you mean?" Her senses returning, Haley raised a sarcastic eyebrow.

He grinned sheepishly.

She relaxed, her gaze sweeping upward to study her pet with affectionate resignation. "Yeah, that's him. He's a little rowdy with guests, so I usually confine him when I have company."

"Aw, let the poor guy out."

She eyed him doubtfully.

"So maybe he'll jump on me a little or slobber all over the place." He shrugged. "I can take it. Want me to let him out?"

"Go for it, but don't say I didn't warn you." She watched in expectant glee as Rick loped up the stairs and fumbled with the gate before finally removing the barrier.

With a joyful bark and a romp, the dog planted both paws on Rick's stomach. With a surprised woof of his own, Rick doubled over and stumbled down a step or two. His chest heaved as he worked to regain the breath the dog had forced from his lungs.

Giggling, Haley watched as Sherlock leaped down the stairs, then ran right back up them. He paused to jump and slobber and whine for the sheer joy of a new-found companion. Then he bounded back down the steps. Before the dog could leap up them again, Rick grabbed the dog's collar with a practiced hand. "Sherlock. Down."

Her giggles dwindled to a disbelieving chuckle as she watched her incorrigible puppy sit and stare, unmoving even after Rick released the leather collar. When Sherlock's rump started to bounce right back off the floor, Rick employed the same, firm tone. "No. Down." The rump hit the floor again. Sherlock cocked his head in curiosity.

Feeling her own head cock with similar emotions, Haley just stared.

After a long moment, Rick patted the puppy on his silky head and fell to his knees in front of him. "Good dog. Way to go, boy." He scrubbed and tugged at the dog's ears until the animal slid to the floor, a boneless mass of ecstasy.

Rick laughed and gave the dog a last pat, then rose to his feet.

"That's incredible. How'd you do that?" Haley glanced back and forth between dog and man. Her shock gave way to irritation that her own pet would obey this stranger before he'd listen to his devoted mistress.

Rick shrugged, his smile easy. "I'm good with dogs. Sherlock here is just a pup, and he's got a lot of heart. He just needs a firm voice and consistency. So, ready for dinner? I'm starved." He shoved his hands in his back pockets. The posture stretched the denim taut across his hips, emphasizing his flat belly and the fullness behind his zipper.

Wrenching her eyes from the sight, Haley swallowed hard and tried for a breezy smile. "Kitchen's in there." The direction was basically moot, since the first floor of her apartment was one big room, divided only by the flow of furniture. And the pizza was already sitting on the kitchen table.

"Great." Rick moved into the kitchen area. A docile Sherlock padded along behind him then dropped down on a braided rug for a nap. Rick casually glanced at an antique teddy bear collection arranged above cabinets painted a cheerful yellow. Smiling at some inner thought, he turned his attention back to the pizza box.

Haley joined him in the kitchen, careful to sidle around the table so it was always positioned between her body and Rick's. "So, um, have a seat."

"Thanks." Rick dropped easily into a chair and flipped open the pizza lid. While Haley lifted a piece out, strings of cheese dangling from the slice, Rick popped the tops of two beers and slid one across the table to her. "I wasn't sure what you liked, so I just ordered a garbage pizza. I figured you could pick off anything that you didn't want."

"Mmm, no. This is great." She sank her teeth into the loaded-down slice, thankful for the distraction of food.

Once they were both satisfied, leaning back comfortably in their chairs, Haley grinned lazily at Rick. "Thanks for the pizza."

Ah, pizza, the great equalizer, she mused silently. Watching each other slurp dangling strings of cheese and lick tomato sauce off fingers tended to knock down any barriers to communication. No longer intimidated, she felt downright benevolent. In that mode, she gave way to her curiosity about the man seated in her kitchen, a stranger to her until just a few days ago.

"So, neighbor, tell me about yourself. Are you new in town or just new to the building?"

"Just new to the building." His face was curiously blank.

"Are you native to the St. Louis area?"

He shook his head. "I grew up in Chicago and moved here about five years ago."

"Chicago, huh? And so you moved here to work at a bike shop?" She gave him a puzzled look.

He paused. "That's right. I like St. Louis. Is that a problem?"

"No, of course not." She shrugged. "I guess you just strike me as a little more cerebral than the average jock. I thought maybe..." She gave him a speculative look.

He returned the look. "You thought that maybe...?"

"Well, I just wondered if you had other ambitions. I mean, I'm sure a bike shop's a lot of fun, but..."

"But?" His smile was even more challenging.

She studied him, then tried a smile. "But nothing, really. I was just curious. We are playing get to know your neighbor, right?"

"Right." He relaxed back in his chair, but his eyes were still alert. "So, neighbor, what about you?"

"Well, you know about the toy shop."

His smile widened. "I like your toy shop."

"Thanks." She relaxed, her smile easier.

"So are you from here originally, then?"

"Born and bred in the area. Although there are days when I think I could easily be convinced to move to Timbuktu." She made a face. "My mother...worries." Remembering her harsh words earlier that day, and a telephoned apology that didn't quite make up for it, she felt a tug at her heart. "She worries a lot, actually."

"I see." His smile widened. "And should she?"

Haley cocked her head, thinking, then grinned. "Well, now that you mention it..." She waved off the idea before continuing in a more serious tone. "No, not really. I'm pretty tame. Not all that bright sometimes." She paused, reflecting briefly on her erstwhile boyfriend and various dates who'd been just like him. "But probably not dangerous to others."

"Just dangerous to yourself," Rick surmised, nodding. "I guess you're referring to your love life?"

She looked down at the napkin she'd begun to shred. "What makes you say that?"

"Oh, probably something to do with your geek-hunting project. And that nauseating conversation I overheard at the computer store today."

She scowled at him. "I thought we were calling a truce, *neighbor*."

"Truce or no truce, you can't just leave me hanging."

"Oh, I don't know. I think I could leave you hanging very easily." She stared pointedly at him.

Rick laughed. "By my neck at the end of a rope, you mean?"

"It's sounding awfully tempting, yes."

"For such a little thing, you can be pretty blood-thirsty." Rick's eyes glinted with mischief. He opened his mouth, no doubt intending to provoke her further.

The screech of her chair sliding back from the table cut off whatever he might have said. She smiled determinedly. "I guess we're through here." She stood up and folded the empty pizza box over, dropping empty cans and dirty napkins on top of it. Balancing the mass, she turned to dump it into the trash. "Well, Rick. It's been fun. I'm sorry you had to leave so suddenly, but I understand how things can be. Don't be a stranger. Really." She smiled winningly at him, hoping he'd simply follow her lead.

Ignoring the verbal shove toward the door, he sat back in his chair and folded his hands over a flat belly. "If you won't explain, I guess I'll just have to draw some conclusions on my own. Let's see. You recently broke up with the boyfriend. So he's out of the picture, leaving you available. So now you've begun hunting geeks as potential replacements. The only question is, why? Why target geeks and why be so single-minded about the hunt? You don't strike me as malicious or twisted, despite my first impression of you. At least not *too* twisted."

He grinned at the glare she tossed him, pausing to allow for interruption. She remained stubbornly silent.

He continued. "So I figure you're either trying to

prove a point or you intend to use the guy in some way."

He touched a knuckle to his mouth. "A wedding or a reunion maybe and you need a date. Fast. A replacement for the fiancé you bragged about. Someone you can introduce around respectably and drop later with no strings or complications." He leaned back farther, gesturing widely with open hands. "Hey, no problem. Give the geeks a break. I'm available and willing. Semi-respectable. Why don't you let me take you to the function, whatever it is." He was obviously impressed with his own logic.

"Wrong. But I'll give you credit for imagination."

She picked up a washcloth and wet it before turning to wipe down the table. To distract herself from Rick's disturbing questions and his even more disturbing presence, she turned her attention to a piece of cheese that had adhered to the table. After a few moments of vigorous scrubbing, she turned back and surprised Rick in the act of staring intently at her rear end. He looked up almost immediately, his eyes innocently wide, but she glared, her cheeks hot.

He cleared his throat, obviously hiding a grin. "Okay. So there's no wedding or reunion. Maybe you just want a harmless, safe date. How about me? I'm thirty-two, unattached, pretty harmless, and I've been told I'm a fun date." He flashed a boyish smile.

"Thank you for the invitation, but no. I don't want to date you."

He managed to look hurt. "What's wrong with dating me? I shower regularly. I've never been convicted of a crime. I can even be pretty entertaining when I put my mind to it."

She sighed and stopped tidying up her kitchen. She faced Rick squarely. "It's not personal, okay? You're an attractive guy, and I'm sure you could get a date any day of the week. I just don't date your type anymore."

"My type? What type am I?"

She slapped the dishcloth on the counter, frustrated. *"You're good-looking."*

He grinned in surprised delight. "You think so? How about that. I decided you were pretty cute the first time I saw you. A little weird maybe, but really cute. It was the freckles, I think. I've always had a thing for them."

Talk about backhanded compliments. "Thank you," she bit out. "Now if we're through with dinner and the getting-acquainted business, I really have a lot to do tonight. So—"

He stood up and followed her back to the sink. "Wait. What about that date?"

Haley's hands fisted. "We're not going on any dates. I told you that already. I'm sorry if this offends you. It has nothing to do with you personally. Got it?"

"Okay, give me the impersonal reason, then." Rick looked immeasurably reasonable.

Haley closed her eyes, her cheeks hot with embarrassment and anger. "It's *because* you're good-looking." The words were carefully enunciated, spoken slowly as though for the ears of a toddler. She opened her eyes and stared at him, dead on, willing him to comprehend. "I won't date you because you're good-looking. I've sworn off hunks, studs, charmers, all of them."

Rick's ego was obviously inflating. "And I qualify? I'm flattered."

She smiled evilly. "Rick, at this point in time, you more than qualify for the group of men I'm trying to avoid. So now that I've answered your question, would you kindly leave?" She tucked the rest of the six-pack under his arm and firmly steered him out the door.

"Goodbye, Rick." She closed and latched the door against him.

Rick stood outside for a moment, thoughtful. His first impression of Haley had been of a sexy maniac. Sure, he'd been distracted for a moment by those freckles on her pert little nose. It was hard not to wonder if she had freckles all over that tight little body, like tiny invitations on creamy skin that never saw the sun...

Clearing his throat and glancing up and down the hallway uncomfortably, Rick turned to unlock his apartment door.

Freckles aside, once he'd seen the incriminating list on Haley's clipboard, he'd felt compelled to intercede. Still did, in fact. And that was why he kept asking her out, although he'd admit that not all of his reasons were altruistic. Hell, he was flat-out attracted to her and wanted to date her for that reason alone.

Given what he'd observed so far, he really doubted that she was the malicious type, just misguided. That didn't mean, however, that she wouldn't end up hurting one of these guys she was targeting. Even if it was by accident. And they already took enough flak from the socially acceptable world without also having to deal with Haley's idiosyncrasies and possible slip-ups.

Rick knew exactly what it was like to be the butt of insensitive comments and pranks. For a good portion of his life, he'd been sadly underweight, nearsighted and socially awkward. He'd grown out of most of the awkwardness, thanks to cycling, contact lenses and professional success.

Closing the door behind him, Rick tossed his keys on the coffee table and headed into the kitchen to stow the beer in the fridge. Opening one and taking a swig, he paused to look out the window at the playground beyond. He heard the faint echo of children squealing and laughing. As always, there was one child who held himself back from the crowd, sitting on one of the benches that lined the periphery of the park.

Rick frowned, his thoughts still forming. No, he didn't think Haley was out to deliberately hurt anyone. Still, he couldn't quite stomach the way she was picking and choosing her dates like she might shop for a new pair of shoes.

She was acting like those women who telephoned him for flimsy reasons or made brazen passes just because they'd heard his name mentioned on local TV. He still couldn't believe it. They'd actually run a story on the town's Top Ten Bachelors...like presenting a menu for the desperately lonely and desperately acquisitive. As much as he could feel for the lonely women in this town, he had no intention of sacrificing himself to the cause.

Just his luck, a local gossip columnist had updated the news of his highly rated bachelor status—to include, among other things, detailed information about his new apartment. So now, despite his discretionary efforts, he had a few of them ambushing him at home, too.

Grinning ruefully, Rick went into the living room to slump down into the couch. The irony of the situation hadn't escaped him. All these women he didn't want chased him because he'd lost the geek trappings and achieved financial success. Haley, on the other hand, turned him on despite her wrongheaded notions, but rejected him because he wasn't a geek. A guy couldn't win for trying.

"RICK, LINE TWO."

"Hello?" Rick spoke absently into the phone, still tapping away at the keyboard.

"You sound like you have your nose pressed against a computer screen again." The feminine voice was indulgently amused.

He grinned and sat back in his chair, folding his free arm across his chest. "And so what if I do? It is my livelihood, Mom."

"I know, honey. But I thought you'd be spending a little more time at that bike shop of yours. You need more variety in your life."

"I manage to fit in a day or two each week at the bike shop, but I can't afford more than that right now. I'm still looking for a manager to handle things here. Once I have someone in place, this store will run itself, just like the Chicago store does, and the one over in Springfield. Then I can spend more time at the bike shop."

"I guess that makes sense."

"So how are the girls?" He had six sisters, all younger, all stairsteps in age. It was enough to give any older brother gray hair before his time.

His mother laughed. "They're doing fine, honey. Even if their brother isn't within bullying distance."

He grinned. "Good. You can tell Stephanie I'll be home for Rowan's birthday party next month. It's not every day a kid turns five."

"Oh, good. They'll be thrilled to hear that. Are you bringing anyone with you?" Her voice was deliberately casual.

He pictured huge brown eyes and a freckled nose, wrinkled in disapproval. *Not likely.* "Probably not."

"Well, it will be nice to have you home for a bit. So how is your new apartment? You still haven't invited me over to see it."

He shrugged easily. "Nothing to see really. It's small, like I told you. Discreet. You know I'm probably not going to stay here very long. I'll buy something a little more comfortable once all this gossip dies down."

"Yes, I know. You told me. But, you're not...*terribly* uncomfortable right now, are you?"

"No. Of course not. It's actually a decent building. People are nice."

"So exactly how small is your apartment?"

"Big enough for me."

"Big enough for a visitor, too?"

Rick paused. "What kind of visitor?"

A gusty sigh sounded over the phone line. "Gregory."

"Not again. Honestly, I can't keep finding the guy

jobs. He's a wonder with computers, but he has absolutely no work ethic."

"But he is your cousin, honey. I thought you were on pretty good terms."

Rick closed his eyes, knowing he'd be admitting defeat at some point in the next five minutes. His mother was a gentle, sweet-talking steamroller. His lips quirked reluctantly. "Greg and I get along fine. When he's working for someone else."

"This time he sounds like he really wants to support himself. And get out of his mother's house. It's getting a little crowded now that his sister and her family have moved back home, too. Greg has potential. You've said so yourself."

"Maybe."

"Come on, Rick. It won't hurt you to give him another shot. I think he's matured a lot in the past year."

"All right, all right. I'm sure I'm going to regret this. Send him out here."

"Oh, good. He'll be arriving in three weeks."

Rick sat forward in his chair, eyes narrowed suspiciously. "Three weeks? Sounds like he already has his plans set. Pretty sure of me, aren't you?"

"You're a good son. I knew you'd help out."

"Mostly because I haven't been given much of a choice," he grumbled, checking his calendar.

"Now, you don't mean that, honey." Her voice overrode any reluctance on his part. "Listen, he'll be there on the eighteenth, sometime in the afternoon. Please be home to meet him. I'm sure he's going to feel awkward about all this."

"How long is he going to stay this time?"

"Oh, dear. My bread's burning."

Rick heard the sound of an oven door opening, flustered feminine noises, and a hasty "I love you" and "goodbye."

When the dial tone grew loud in his ear, Rick shook his head and replaced the receiver. "I don't know why Greg would feel awkward about showing up on my doorstep. He should be used to it by now." Glancing at his watch, Rick sighed and logged off the computer.

As he strode out to his car, Rick mentally prepared himself for the prospect of having his home invaded by an irresponsible, lazy slob. Sure, Greg had a good heart, but for a grown man, he still acted like an immature teenager.

It didn't help that everyone made excuses for Greg's faults. His whole family indulged him as though he were still a pimply sixteen-year-old. Probably because he looked like one. Greg's skinny build was much like his own had been as an adolescent, and he wore hauntingly familiar thick glasses and ill-fitting clothes.

Rick shook his head. Setting aside Greg's irresponsibility and questionable ethics, Rick couldn't help feeling some empathy toward his cousin. Something in the genes seemed to predispose all the men in his family to physical awkwardness and computer proficiency. In short, they were all nerds. Dorks. Geeks. Hell, if only Haley could see—

Rick froze, eyes widening at the opportunity that suddenly presented itself.

He couldn't. Could he?

4

"Hey, Aunt Haley!"

"Christopher, hi." She finished locking her door then turned to smile at the little boy.

He frowned back, eyeing the unusually conservative outfit she'd donned for a trip to a local copy center. She needed to make copies of sale flyers, and on the off chance that Rick's silly suggestion held any merit, she had dressed appropriately. Or so she'd thought.

The little boy wrinkled his nose. "You look funny."

Haley raised an eyebrow at the little guy, ignoring a twinge of discomfort. This outfit must be really different from her usual style if even a six-year-old could tell the difference. She'd set aside her usual vivid colors and daring styles and had tried instead for harmless and approachable. It was just possible that she'd overshot the mark. "Well, gee, you look pretty funny yourself."

The responding grin she'd expected never appeared. Instead, a tiny line creased his forehead and he stared down at his shoes.

"Hey, what's wrong, Chris?" She dropped to a knee to look into his little face.

He shrugged, keeping his eyes downcast.

"Wait, let me guess. You didn't eat your green beans again and your mom took away computer privileges."

He shook his head.

"You didn't eat your computer, so your mom took away green bean privileges?"

He shook his head again, but Haley was relieved to see his lips twitch a bit at her foolishness.

"Your turtle ate your green beans and now he's hogging all your computer time?"

A smile threatened, then finally spread across his little face. His eyes met hers. "You're silly."

"You always say that." She smiled at him, hugged him quick. "So spill the green beans. Did something happen at school today? How do you like your new teacher?"

"Mrs. Simpson's okay." His sigh was gusty with the melodrama of youth. "But the other kids were making fun of me. Cuz I'm short."

"Ah. That used to happen to me, too, and it really hurt my feelings."

He nodded.

"Know what I used to do when kids made fun of me because of my size?"

"What?"

She grinned, eyes narrowed. "Why, I just made 'em laugh. Everybody likes to laugh and when they're laughing and thinking you're funny, they don't worry about how tall you are. Know any good jokes?"

He cocked his head with interest. "Well, maybe one, but that's only because I heard one of the kids telling it at school. And he told everyone, so they already know the funny part."

Haley nodded, then motioned him closer. "Tell you

what. There's this really cool joke book at my store. I think you'd like it."

"Really?"

"Really. And, since you're a personal friend of mine, I might be willing to cut you a deal." She nodded slyly.

He moved closer. "Like what?"

"Well, Sherlock's fur needs to be brushed regularly, and since I'm a grown-up it's hard for me to get down low enough to brush his chest and belly. If you come over and brush him for me whenever your mom says it's okay, then I'll give you the book. Fair trade. What do you say?" She held out her hand.

Christopher's eyes sparkled. He adored Sherlock. "Deal!" He shook her hand enthusiastically.

Standing up, she ruffled his hair. "Okay. Just talk to your mom first and make sure it's okay."

"I will." He took off down the hallway.

Haley watched him, her smile bittersweet. Childhood was tough.

"You handled that well."

Haley whirled around to face Rick. He was eyeing her oddly.

"You were listening in. Again. Do you eavesdrop on everyone or just me?"

"To be honest, I think I've taken a personal interest in eavesdropping on you. I'm still trying to figure you out." He shook his head, a reluctant grin tugging at his lips.

"Take all the time you need. In fact, I'll leave you alone so you can focus your undivided attention on analyzing my twisted behavior." She flashed him a tight smile before turning smartly and walking down the hallway. The sharp clicking of sensible flats marked her quick, neat steps.

Rick watched her retreating form, staring long after she'd disappeared around the corner to go down the stairs. He hadn't lied. No way could he figure the woman out. Just when he thought he had a handle on her character, she went and shifted again on him.

Like now, for instance. She'd been unusually sensitive, even clever in her handling of the little boy. It was hard to reconcile this side of her with the woman who was setting out to trap her own personal geek. How could she be so sensitive in one respect, but so blind in another? And she went to such lengths to be blind, too.

As far as he could see, she'd even gone so far as to change her style of dress. Was she trying for conservative? If so, she really ought to check out the rear view, because that simple little skirt did very complicated things across the sweet curves of her behind. He only hoped he could keep his distance from her long enough to determine which woman was the real Haley.

RICK WHEELED HIS BIKE SLOWLY down the hallway to his apartment. He'd ridden his bike at five-thirty every evening for a week and a half—the same time he'd seen Haley wheeling hers up to her apartment that first time. So far, his stratagem hadn't paid off. So much for subtlety.

After parking his bike in the extra bedroom and grabbing a piece of misdirected junk mail, Rick decisively left his apartment and walked over to Haley's door, ringing the doorbell. He grinned at the telltale bark and skitter of toenails on linoleum.

"Wait, Sherlock. No!" A curse, a distinctive splash, and then a low mumbling of frustration followed. Finally, the front door opened, and there stood Haley, dripping all over her own doormat. She peered out at him from beneath a dripping skein of reddish-brown hair. "Hello, Rick," she greeted him with exaggerated patience.

Rick nodded, grimacing. "Haley. How are you?"

"Other than dripping wet," she paused to frown at the puppy poking his bone-dry face between her leg and the front door, "just fine. What can I do for you?"

He glanced at the envelope in his hand. One of his less subtle strategies, and certainly badly timed, but it was all he had right now. He held it out. "Well, I just dropped by to—"

A loud barking interrupted them, followed by a blurry streak of chocolate-colored fur as Sherlock shot out the door and after a fluffy white Persian.

"Sherlock, wait!" Haley lunged to go after the dog.

Noticing her bare feet, Rick grabbed her arm to stop her. "No, I'll get him." He absently thrust the envelope in her hand, then took off down the hallway and loped down the stairs.

Hearing a yowl, followed by a bark-yip-*yipe*, Haley squeezed her eyes shut. Then she heard the distant clatter of aluminum against aluminum, against pavement...a masculine yell. "Oh, no. Not again." She winced. It was trash day, she remembered, and Sherlock had an unhealthy affinity for trash cans and their smelly contents.

A few moments later, Rick reappeared, a bedraggled Sherlock looking chastened and properly obedient as he walked at Rick's heel. Haley clapped a hand over her mouth. "Oh, Rick, no."

"Oh, Haley, yes." His smile was strained. His pants and arms were smeared with what could only be the remains of somebody's dinner. A mostly eaten dinner roll, encrusted with some unidentified green slime hung from Sherlock's furry chest. Lumpy beige gunk, possibly the days-old remainder of somebody's oatmeal, matted the dog's front legs and Rick's shirtsleeve, and part of a soup can label hung from Rick's shoulder. A withered slice of orange rind and part of a banana peel clung to Rick's thigh. Obviously, they'd toured the row of trash cans thoroughly.

After the visual survey, Haley looked up to meet the carefully blank expression in Rick's eyes.

"I believe this is yours?" He dragged forth the filthy, cowering pup.

Lips quivering with the strain of *not* laughing, Haley gripped Sherlock's collar. She watched as Rick turned with careful dignity to go back to his apartment. Biting her lip, she managed to control her reaction until both apartment doors were safely closed between them. Then she bent over double, giggling until the tears streamed down her cheeks. Sherlock barked and made a lunge for her laughing face.

"Oh, no. You've got to be kidding. To the tub with you. And this time *you're* getting the bath, not me." Still shaken with the occasional chuckle, she led the smelly animal directly to the bathroom and kicked the door shut behind them.

AN HOUR LATER, RICK OPENED the door to a freshly groomed pair. With a firm grip on Sherlock's leash, Haley flashed a winning smile and extended a peace offering. "I thought you might prefer it a little fresher this time?" Threatening laughter sparkled in her eyes.

Rick's eyes narrowed, but he accepted the beribboned willow basket she handed him. It was piled high with fresh oranges and bananas. On top of the mound of fruit, displayed for maximum impact, she'd propped an unopened can of soup. After a moment, Rick sighed and shook his head, an unwilling grin twisting his lips. He motioned her inside.

Chuckling openly, Haley guided her dog past him and into the apartment. She looked around curiously. Following her gaze, he wondered what she thought of the place. It was comfortable, but unquestionably masculine, with sturdy hardwood furniture, simple lines and dark colors. Quite a change from her teddy bears, antiques and cheerful yellow cabinets, he thought with a smile. He wondered what color she'd paint this room if given the chance.

After a moment, Haley turned back to face Rick, her smile apologetic. "I'm really sorry about earlier." She shot a stern glance at the sweet-smelling dog. Sherlock gazed back with a panting doggy smile and a wag of the tail. "What a rotten reward for going after this crazy mutt for me."

Rick rolled his eyes. "No pun intended, I hope."

"Ouch. Actually, no." She grinned. "But seriously—"

Rick waved off her stumbling apologies with a grin.

"Don't worry about it." He glanced down at her scamp of a dog. "I think we decided it was the cat's fault."

Haley clucked her tongue, a teasing glitter in her eyes. "Have you ever noticed the amazing similarities between canine logic and male logic?"

"Hey, it only makes sense. *Man's* best friend, remember?" He grinned right back at her. "So why don't you have a seat. Can I get you anything to drink?"

"Oh, that's all right. I was just stopping by quick—"

Rick gave her a stern look and gently nudged her toward the couch. "If you just drop off the basket and run, I'm gonna have to take offense. I waded through garbage for you and this mutt of yours. I think that entitles me to a few minutes of your time."

Haley grinned, no doubt relishing the vision of him and Sherlock wallowing in refuse.

"I don't think I trust that smile of yours."

She laughed.

His own smile deepened as he watched her whole face light up with amusement. Freckled noses should always wrinkle so attractively above a huge smile, he decided. He wondered if Tim would appreciate that freckled nose as much as he did.

"So, what's new with the guy from the computer store?" Rick kept his face carefully devoid of expression.

She shrugged. "Nothing you don't already know. We have a date tomorrow night."

Rick went to the fridge and pulled out two colas. He held one up in question. At Haley's nod, he opened it and handed it to her. He plopped down on the couch beside her and reached down to scratch Sherlock's head. The dog, who'd been leaning adoringly against Haley's shin, craned his neck toward Rick's scratching fingers.

"No comment?" Haley asked, her voice challenging.

He shrugged and sat back in the couch to look at her. "Would it do any good?"

"No."

Whining pathetically, Sherlock clambered onto the couch and draped himself across Rick's lap for more scratching. Rick absently obliged.

When he only stared without further comment, Haley dropped her head back against the sofa cushions to stare at the ceiling. "Look, Rick. I don't know why you find all this so offensive. I'm not a scam artist or some Black Widow type. I'm just dating. Very simple."

"But so calculated." He continued to study her.

She raised her head to frown at him. "So what? I've stumbled along up to this point and ended up a loser every time. This time, I'm taking control, thinking things through. There's nothing wrong with that. I'm just learning from past mistakes."

One eyebrow lifted. "Like the ex-boyfriend?"

"All right, yes. Just like him. He was one of my bigger mistakes, but I've dated a lot of mistakes like him. Unfaithful, self-centered, inconsiderate. All they had going for them was charm and good looks. This time, I'm going for steady, attentive and loyal. I'm tired of jerks who put on a show of being passionately in love with me when they're really only in love with themselves."

Rick tugged gently at Sherlock's ears. "I think I see

what you're getting at, but I have to tell you. I think you're going about all this the wrong way."

"You sound like Jen." At his questioning glance, she explained. "My business partner. A friend."

"Right." He nodded, remembering the pleasant-faced woman at the toy shop. "So she thinks your geek-hunting plan sounds off base, too?"

Haley shot him a narrow look.

"Come on. I heard the line of bull you were feeding that poor guy at the computer store. You were putting on an act just to get a date."

"I was just being nice." Her voice rose indignantly.

"Exactly my point."

She slugged his shoulder and he grinned down at her.

"Seriously, Haley, you've got to realize that being a social outcast doesn't guarantee the guy's a decent person. There are all kinds of jerks in this world."

She sighed and slumped back in the couch. "Maybe. But this is the plan for now. I can always change course if things don't work out."

And so far, she had to admit, the plan wasn't exactly blazing any new trails for her. Computer guy Tim was her only viable new prospect. Despite her tedious wardrobe preparations, the copy shop had been a complete bust, although she'd gotten her fliers copied, thanks to the help of the lone woman manning the store.

"A possible change of course. Sounds promising." His voice warmed with interest. "So what do you have in mind for a Plan B?"

"None of your business." She glanced down at her

dog, frowning to see him sprawled across Rick's lap, soft underbelly exposed for caressing fingers. Shameless whimpers of pleasure escaped his velvety snout. "And what have you done to my dog, anyway? Sherlock?"

The dog merely glanced at her before nuzzling Rick's hand into continuing that marvelous scratching. Haley's gaze was riveted to those scratching fingers, so tender and knowledgeable. *Mmm. Lucky Sherlock.* She forcibly averted her eyes.

Rick laughed when the dog snuffled and started licking his hand. "Hey, your dog likes me. Shouldn't that be one of those good signs you look for in a guy? One who gets along well with animals and children?"

Ignoring the traitorous skipping beat of her own heart, Haley smiled evilly. "Sure. Those are great qualities. Every woman looks for them in a prospective *husband*. It helps her see what sort of father he's going to be. From the looks of things now, I'd say you're about ready for the altar. Gonna marry Sherlock?"

He frowned in mock seriousness, unfazed by the matrimonial references. "No, but we might date casually for a while. Does he have a curfew?"

"You're so twisted." She chuckled reluctantly.

"So I've been told." He shifted to tug on the dog's ears, eliciting a true groan from the animal.

"You're disgustingly good with him."

Rick smiled, his eyes still on the dog. "Comes with experience. We always had a couple of dogs running around when I was growing up. This guy's going to be great. Smart, spirited, bighearted. He just needs to learn some manners and obey commands."

"Oh, is that all?" She widened her eyes in mock wonderment, then snorted. "Maybe you ought to try training this horse of a dog. He's cute, sure, but cute just doesn't cut it when he's chewing on my clothes, eating my furniture and ruining the carpet."

Rick paused in his scratching then, at Sherlock's protest, resumed more slowly. "Okay. When should we start?"

She stared in surprise. "You're kidding."

"No, really. I'm good with dogs."

"But why do you want to train *my* dog?"

He turned serious eyes on her. "Maybe to show you not all guys are jerks like the ones you've dated."

She paused, studying him softly, while inwardly trying to deny the sincerity in his gaze. It would be so easy to believe…to try… She shook it off and forced a casual reply. "But I already know that."

He raised an eyebrow. "Sure you do. You just think a guy has to be— What'd you call it? A *frog*? As opposed to your cheating prince of an ex?" He shook his head. "I don't get it. Can you honestly believe a guy has to be ugly and socially inept in order to be a decent human being?"

She responded with a self-deprecating grin. "No, not really. I just think my odds are better that way. My judgment is notoriously bad where men are concerned. And I've begun to believe it's because I see a hot body or a handsome face instead of what's inside a man. Take away the hot body and handsome face and there won't be anything to distract me, right?"

Rick stared. "So you want to eliminate all sexual attraction from the equation. That's nuts, Haley. How are you going to make it in the bedroom if you're not even remotely turned on by the guy?" *And what a crying shame that would be.* He couldn't imagine all that energy and passion going untapped, untested. Damn, if she'd just give him a chance to show her how good they'd be—

Haley shook her head, her cheeks rosy and her eyes evasive. "Let's just agree to disagree on this point, shall we? And thanks for the offer to help with Sherlock, but I can't ask that of you. We'll struggle through on our own for a while. Right, dog?"

Still blissfully moaning and whimpering, the dog didn't bother to acknowledge her comment.

"Come on, Sherlock."

With a last moan, the pup turned a baleful stare on his mistress. Sighing, Haley tugged at his collar, and he finally gave in to the pressure, stepping off Rick's lap and letting himself be dragged toward the door.

"Let me know if you change your mind." Rick stood up, watching in amused concern as Haley struggled with her dog. Given a few months, the animal would probably outweigh her.

"Well, Rick, it's been interesting. Thanks for the soda. Oh, and thanks for rescuing Sherlock here. Looks like you've got a friend for life."

"Really?" Rick's eyes were steady on hers.

"Stop it. We're not dating."

"You're breaking my heart." He grinned.

Not deigning to respond, Haley turned and headed toward the door.

Watching the door close behind her, Rick considered

her thoughtfully. No, she wasn't heartless. Misguided, maybe, but not heartless. He could work with that.

THE NEXT DAY, HALEY DELIGHTED in relating to Jen, blow by blow, Rick and Sherlock's adventures with the cat and garbage. Jen laughed long and helplessly. Still holding her sides, she shook her head. "Oh, Haley. You've just got to give this guy a chance."

"Says who?"

"Says me. And says you, too, if you could only see your face when you talk about him."

"Surely you're not suggesting that I've fallen for Rick now. I mean, sure he's hot—totally makes my knees melt, if you want to know the truth. He's even fun to hang out with now that I've gotten to know him a little better. But that's as far as I can let things go with him. He's way too good-looking—women just crawl all over him."

Jen rolled her eyes.

"No, seriously, Jen, you wouldn't believe the number of times I've heard a woman knocking on his door at some strange hour. I guess they just can't get enough of him." Suppressing her jealous musings, Haley moved on to his most telling offense. "The man is smooth. Lethally smooth." She stared meaningfully at her friend.

"Maybe. I've only met the guy once. He may very well be slime. Like you, though, I'm not sure I trust your judgment when it comes to men."

Jen stood up and reached into a box she'd set on the floor. She began pulling out stuffed frogs, lizards, snakes and dinosaurs. One by one, she unwrapped them and arranged them on the display. In the middle of fluffing up a flattened iguana, Jen froze and looked up. "Hey, why don't you arrange for me to talk to him again? That way, I'll be able to put in my two cents' worth based on a little firsthand knowledge."

"I don't think that's necessary." Haley pulled out a stack of picture books and arranged them on a shelf in the preschoolers' section.

"Oh, come on. What could it hurt?"

"And would Frank want you hanging around my building to meet men?" Haley teased, hoping to distract her friend.

Jen ignored Haley's remark. "I promise I'll just be friendly. I won't even ask him if he's seeing anyone right now."

"You're damn right you won't. Forget it. I'm not dating him. He's my neighbor and a potential—but purely *platonic*—friend. End of story."

"Spoilsport," Jen grumbled. "So, are you ready for your hot date tonight?"

Haley smiled ruefully. "Feeling vengeful, are we? Yes, I'm ready. And—unlike some of us—I'm still trying to keep an open mind about Tim. He was pleasant and helpful at the computer store, and we had a nice conversation on the phone last night. I'm sure I'll have a very nice evening."

Jen raised an eyebrow but didn't comment.

THE HOT DATE BOMBED.

It wasn't because Tim was annoying or offensive, she realized. He wasn't. He was a decent, thoughtful person. Wonderful husband material, in fact.

For someone else.

He took her to a trendy little Greek restaurant he'd never before patronized. But it showed he was willing to enjoy new experiences, which had to be a good sign. So she smiled when he held the door for her and stood aside while he gave their names to the hostess.

The wait for their table was endless, something for which no reasonable person would hold him responsible, and yet—

"Man, I'm so sorry about this, Haley." Apologizing for what felt to her like the twentieth time in as many minutes, Tim glanced around feverishly and consulted his watch yet again. Nervous perspiration dotted his forehead and his glasses kept sliding down his impressive length of shiny nose. "Maybe we could try someplace else or I could— What if I tipped the hostess a little more...?" He glanced around, nearly stood up.

"No. *Really.*" Haley forced her strained smile up a notch. "It's okay. I promise. We'll just sit here at the bar and relax. No rush, right?"

"Uh, right. Yeah." He glanced around still, and Haley couldn't help but notice the rapidly growing circles under his armpits. *Eeeewww.* If he'd just keep his arms down, maybe—

She cleared her throat and slapped that smile back on her face. "So, Tim, tell me about yourself. What do you like to do? Any driving ambitions?" She deliberately made her tone playful, despite the driving urge to flee in self-preservation.

He blinked, slowly lowered his arms and cleared his throat. "Well, I-I'm in my third year at St. Louis University, and..."

"Oh, that's great." Her voice sounded faint to her own ears. She barely kept her smile in place. *Third year?* Should he be drinking?

He shrugged and gave a halfhearted grin. "Well, I should be a couple years further than that, but I took some time off."

She nodded encouragingly, recalculated his age and the likelihood of running into liquor patrol or an enraged mommy, then settled in to listen. A long, laborious thirty minutes later, the hostess called their names.

Once they were seated, Haley sighed and ordered a simple plate of gyros from the menu. Tim did the same. That's when the real trial began. Maybe he was nervous or maybe he just feared the evening would lapse into uncomfortable silence. Whatever the reason, Tim talked fast and seemingly without breathing. His subject matter was limited to computers and the computer science degree he hoped to obtain.

"So you're planning a career in computer science. That sounds exciting. Challenging." Haley gave him an encouraging nod, watched his cheeks flush with pride, then continued in a gentle voice. "So what do you do for fun?"

He grinned even more widely, eyes sparkling like gems as he gestured with sweaty enthusiasm. "Well, there's this new computer game out, and..."

Haley's eyes glazed over again. He really was sweet. Despite the waving, perspiring arms. Genuine even. She bet he'd get along great with Christopher, her kid neighbor.

For more reasons than one. Tim was maybe twenty-three years old to her twenty-eight, and his awkwardness made him seem even younger. That made them five years apart in age, and worlds apart in life experiences and personal interests.

Worse, even Tim could find only so much to say about computers. Once their salads were removed, he seemed to run out of steam, and he tried desperately not to look at her, his eyes wide with panic as he inhaled his gyros by the cheekful.

She could relate. A girl could only glance up and smile pleasantly so many times. Her face was starting to hurt.

When the waitress cleared their table and dropped off the check, Haley silently blessed her while skillfully intercepting.

"Oh, no. My treat. Really." Tim gave her another one of his nervous grins, nearly knocking his water glass over as he reached for the check.

"Tim, that's sweet, but we can split it. You have college to pay for. That's important." She gave him a teasing look that usually worked. "Besides, I'm a modern sort of woman who likes to pay her way, and you look, oh, modern enough to handle something like that."

He laughed and reluctantly agreed.

Afterward, Haley pleaded fatigue and then ended the evening early, both to her relief and his, she was sure.

Still, she wasn't disheartened, Haley decided as she ascended the stairs of her apartment building. True, Tim wasn't the right guy for her and the evening had been uncomfortable. But also true, he was a genuinely nice guy. Perhaps, in some way, she was on the right track.

"Well, hi, Haley. Early evening?" Rick smiled over his shoulder at her. He was crouched in front of her door, a can of WD-40 in his hand as he worked the doorknob.

Haley froze, mentally weaving stories about serial killers and the things they did to unsuspecting neighbors and provoking acquaintances.

"Um, what *exactly* are you doing?"

"Fixing your door. Every time you come home, I hear you rattling around out here trying to get it open. It looked like the manager wasn't getting to it anytime soon, so I thought, why not." He shrugged. "Go ahead and try it. See if it works any better."

Haley eyed him warily, wondering if she should do any such thing.

His brows rose in surprised innocence. "I was just trying to do you a favor." At her continued stare, his expression became a little sheepish. "Oh, all right. It was a good excuse to hang around your door and keep an eye on this date of yours. Make sure he didn't give you any trouble. You know, neighbors looking out for neighbors."

She considered that explanation. Perhaps it wasn't the full truth, but it was probably closer than the fixing-the-door line. "Okay. Well, thanks. I appreciate it." Awkwardly, she juggled her keyring for the right key and inserted it into the lock. It twisted smoothly and the door swung open without protest. "This works great. Thanks, Rick." She stepped inside, then paused before turning back to him. "Would you like to come in? I made some cookies in case..."

"In case loverboy turned out to be Mr. Right?"

Her brows lowered. "In case he— Well, yes. I thought that if we hit it off, I could invite him up for cookies and coffee. *Then send him on his way.*"

Rick nodded, obviously forcing back a grin. "He wasn't cookie-worthy?"

She sighed glumly. "Not even close."

He nodded, wisely refraining from further comment. "Well, I'd hate to let a plate of cookies go unappreciated. Lead me to 'em."

He followed her in and began browsing around her apartment while Haley started the coffee. As she poured water into the coffeemaker, Haley glanced out the window and down at the darkening playground beyond. A last child jumped off the swings and raced off toward the building.

Smiling absently at the sight, Haley remembered what it was like as a kid trying to squeeze every last moment of daylight. Once the coffee was brewing, she went upstairs to free a desperately whining Sherlock. She took the baby gate down, then froze at the sight of her bedroom.

While she'd been gone, Sherlock had used his time to exercise his sharp little teeth. And his bowels. Her lacy curtains were shredded, a suspicious odor emanated from a pile of clothes in the corner and her fourposter bed resembled a mattress supported by wellchewed toothpicks.

When she finally found her voice, Haley shrieked loud enough to send Sherlock cowering in a corner— and Rick leaping up the stairs behind her. She felt him pause behind her before he let out a low whistle that made her want to ram an elbow between his ribs.

"Looks like your dog got bored, Haley. Or jealous. Did loverboy pick you up at the door by any chance?"

She glanced at him over her shoulder, mentally cataloging the damages. "What has that to do with anything?"

"Sherlock considers you his personal property. And your date was poaching. The dog just expressed his disapproval. Thoroughly." Rick's lips twitched as though restraining a grin.

She gave in and sent the elbow where it wanted to go.

He winced and rubbed at his side, his amused expression fading at last as he looked around the room again. Anyone but the most insensitive of fools would realize the dog had ruined some treasured belongings.

Her hands slow with dread, Haley scooted the gate out of her way and cautiously moved into the room. She approached Sherlock, who eyed her pathetically. His tail thumped once, hopefully. She glowered.

Rick approached her from behind. "Why don't you let me take the dog out. That'll give you a chance to take care of the worst of the mess. Unless you'd rather I stay to help."

Stiffening her spine, Haley shook her head. "No, I can clean it up. I suppose it would help, though, if you'd take him outside for a few minutes to take care of business." She glanced back at him briefly. "Thanks."

"No problem." He clipped a leash onto the dog and led him out of the apartment.

Once dog and man had left, Haley quickly located

carpet cleaner, rags and plastic bags. She kicked off her shoes and set to work.

When she pulled a table scarf away to inspect the floor beneath it, she could have cried. There was Raggan, the cheerful little rag doll she used to drag everywhere when she was a child. As an adult, she'd propped the doll in a place of honor, on top of a cedar chest at the foot of her bed. Now, Raggan looked like a mangled pile of rags on the floor. Yellowed cotton stuffing protruded from various holes on her poor, faded body.

Cradling the rag doll in one arm, Haley went back downstairs, glaring at her pet when he bounded through the front door ahead of Rick.

He frowned and approached. "What's wrong?" His gaze dropped to the mangled old doll, which told its own story. As did, no doubt, her inability to hold back a tear or two. Rick gave the dog a stern glance. "Bad Sherlock."

The dog's ears drooped, as did his tail and the lids of his eyes. He dropped to the floor and stared up at them sorrowfully.

Rick turned back to Haley. "I'm sorry about the doll."

She sniffed. "It's okay. I think I can fix her."

He nodded and squeezed her shoulder.

"Um, Rick? Is that offer to help train Sherlock still open? Because if it is, I'll take it. Before you change your mind." She smiled sheepishly, tossing a baleful glance at the dog.

Rick grinned and rubbed a thumb against her cheek, drying her tears.

She started at the unexpected touch, her eyes wide as she met his. After a strained moment, Haley stepped back and glanced down at the doll. She absently began poking tufts of yellowed cotton back into the gaping holes Sherlock had chewed.

Rick cleared his throat. "Look, why don't I finish cleaning up while you change into something more comfortable."

At Haley's pointed stare, he rolled his eyes. "You always think the worst of me. I *meant* for you to get out of those pantyhose and fancy clothes and throw on some sweats or something."

"Right. Sorry." She inhaled, exhaled. "That's actually a good idea. I'll just grab a few things and change in the bathroom."

Feeling awkward and confused over the too intimate moment she'd just shared with Rick, Haley was grateful for the chance to collect herself. She turned and ran up the stairs to her bedroom. Keeping her gaze carefully away from the worst of the mess Sherlock had created, she foraged for a roomy men's dress shirt and pair of leggings before closing herself in the bathroom. Once inside, she held the outfit against her and looked in the mirror. Perfect. Comfortable but not unattractive.

And why did she care if it was attractive or not? she scolded herself as she listened to heavy footsteps coming up the stairs. Was she starting to like this guy? Oh, who was she fooling? What was there not to like?

She frowned as she rolled her pantyhose down her hips and legs then reached for her leggings. She paused as she heard definite sounds coming from the other side of the door. It felt incredibly intimate having a man clean up her bedroom while she changed clothes in the adjoining bathroom. It was exciting in a perverted sort of way, she supposed.

She pictured him dropping to his knees in those tight jeans of his and groaned silently. Why couldn't he wear baggy pants and huge sweatshirts or something equally concealing? No, he had to wear old T-shirts that clung at the biceps and stretched across his broad chest. Oh, and his jeans. Denim faded to a soft white and cradling that incredible behind. The front view of them was such that she had to keep her eyes above waist-level or she risked embarrassing herself with blushes or animalistic panting.

Haley closed her eyes as she buttoned her shirt. What was she doing? Was she really that infatuated with Rick? Wistfully, she wondered if she ought to date him a few times, just to convince herself that like the other princes he was a jerk underneath it all. With enough exposure, she might even get used to his considerable charms and stop being so affected by him.

She opened her eyes. Surely she was strong enough—or at least knowledgeable enough, given their friendship and familiarity with each other as neighbors—to be around him without risking too much up front. Sighing, she listened to the muffled movements outside the bathroom door—the sound of spraying and then a tuneless whistle. How was a woman supposed to resist a man who whistled while he cleaned up her mess?

Silently bracing herself, Haley opened the bathroom

door, a carefully composed smile on her face. "That's much better. Thanks."

Rick stood up and turned, his grin widening as he appraised her outfit. His gaze lingered over the open collar of her shirt and the way the leggings clung to her thighs. The impact of his gaze on her pulse was incredible. "Much better is right." He cleared his throat. "Well, I'm almost done here. How about I meet you downstairs?"

"Um, sure. I'll...check on the coffee." She trotted down the steps, carefully monitoring her pace so she didn't appear to be in full retreat. Even if she was. That man's eyes should not be allowed in any woman's bedroom. Take no prisoners lethal.

After checking on the coffee, she noticed the message light blinking on her answering machine. She hit the play button and as it rewound, she heard Rick jogging lightly down the stairs. He held up the paper towels and cleaning sprays, silently asking where he ought to put everything.

She pointed to the cabinets beneath the sink. As Rick approached, a tinny, masculine voice broke into the quiet of the room.

"*Hi, Haley. This is Peter...*"

5

"HI, HALEY. THIS IS PETER...I'm sorry about the, um...misunderstanding." Pause. Gusty sigh. "Man, this is awkward. Look. I was just wondering if—"

Haley closed her eyes, savoring the exquisite sense of satisfaction. Victory. Anticipation. Peter was going to beg for a second chance. Not that she wanted him back, but it would certainly soothe her battered ego to know he regretted the loss.

"—I could come over and get my tennis racquet. I left it at your place the last time I saw you and, well, it's my lucky racquet. I have this big match coming up, so... Anyway, I'll be by tomorrow around six to pick it up."

A click, a couple of beeps and the answering machine went silent.

Haley considered killing the mechanical messenger. Abruptly, she turned away, then almost jumped when she encountered Rick standing directly behind her. His eyes were watchful.

"The ex, I take it."

Haley nodded.

"Sounds like a winner." His face remained expressionless.

"You don't know the half of it."

Rick nodded slowly. "I see. So there's some satisfaction in making the guy crawl back to you and beg for the lucky racquet."

She smiled slowly, contemplating. "Yes. There is that. You know, I don't think he'll be using his lucky racquet any time soon." Her smile grew evil. "I was a little upset after my last encounter with Peter."

The satisfaction she'd gained from her retaliation via intercom had worn off quickly when she'd come home to find his dirty socks in her laundry room. He'd left them there after his last tennis match, no doubt expecting that she'd wash them for him like a good little girlfriend. She'd gotten angry all over again, until she'd found something else of his propped neatly against the wall....

"Since I didn't have his cheating face for a target," she continued aloud, "I had to find an appropriate substitute. And all I could find was a pretty little tennis racquet. What a shame."

Rick grinned. "What a nasty shame. I'm sure you'll feel terrible to have to tell him his lucky racquet is gone."

She blinked with wide-eyed innocence. "Now why would I tell him any such thing?" She reached into the tiny laundry room and retrieved the broken, twisted mass of wood and string. "I saved it for just such an occasion."

"Wow. Remind me not to piss you off."

She smiled grimly and tossed the racquet back into the laundry room.

Still studying her, Rick settled himself on the couch and folded his arms across his chest. "So, what happened with Peter? Obviously, you two didn't part as friends."

"I thought you were eavesdropping."

"I told you all I heard that day was something about Prince Charming and frogs. Tell me what happened."

She sighed. "No, I wouldn't call it a friendly parting of ways. To make a long story short, I paid him a surprise visit at the office and found his secretary at *his* desk instead of hers."

He looked nonplussed.

"Actually, I should say she was sprawled naked across his desk with him— Well, you get the idea."

"Ouch." Rick frowned.

"Hmm. Yes." She inhaled deeply then blew it out on a determined breath. "So are you ready for those cookies?"

He studied her face through narrow eyes. "I don't think so." At her questioning look, he smiled slightly. "Let's get out of here."

"And go where?"

He frowned a moment in thought, then grinned. "I got it. There's something I've been dying to do since I moved into this building. Come on."

Five minutes later, Haley glanced around at the playground equipment, then back at him. She started laughing. Obviously, they were on the same wavelength.

"You, too, huh?" He grinned, the look in his eyes that of an ecstatic eight-year-old.

"Uh-huh. So bad I considered calling a therapist." With a laugh, Haley made a beeline for the swings, a chuckling Rick following her lead.

"I don't know if these things are going to hold me, Haley."

"Ooh, big man. Are you too solid and studly for mere chains to hold you?" she taunted, already pumping her swing higher and higher.

He swatted her rear on the backswing, before carefully settling into the tire swing next to her. "It's not the chains I'm worried about."

She stuck her tongue out at him.

Accepting it for the challenge that it was, Rick shot her a wicked grin and went for broke. From the swings, Haley raced him to the slide, which he bypassed with an incredulous look. It didn't stand much taller than him and couldn't possibly hold his weight. Besides, he had his sights set farther beyond.

Chuckling, Haley scrambled to the top of the ladder and slid down the curving metal slide, whooping.

"Incorrigible runt." He shook his head, but caught her at the bottom and flipped her over his shoulder. "Portable, though."

Grinning at the small fists pounding him on the back, he hauled her off to the merry-go-round, dumping her on her bottom in the center. He jumped off and began spinning the thing with huge heaves. Haley grinned into the darkness, clearly dazzled.

Once the merry-go-round was spinning easily, he gave the whirling disk one last push and leaped on without disturbing its momentum. He settled against one of the crossbars to enjoy the ride in silence.

Happy and pleasantly tired, Haley lay down with her head in the center and stared up at the dizzying whirl of stars and planets. The moon. It felt magical.

Sensing Rick's eyes on her, Haley glanced toward him. His face was an intriguing play of shadow and light beneath the glow of the moon. She could see a small, appreciative smile tugging at the corners of his mouth.

"This was fun, Rick. Just what I needed." She spoke with quiet sincerity.

His smile faded. "After the boring date and the message from your ex, you mean?"

"Are you trying to start a fight again? Seems a shame to spoil the evening," she noted calmly.

"Just answer the question."

"Like I said, this was fun. Yes, it was more enjoyable than my date—and I'd rather review my tax return than be reminded of my ex."

"So, go out with me. For real. Not a neighborly get-together with all the lines drawn. A real date."

She sat up and drew her knees to her chest, resting her chin on top of them. "A real date. You and me."

"What do you say?" he asked softly.

She felt her no-prince resolve wavering. As much as she hated to admit it, Rick was right in saying she had more fun with him than with Tim. Or anyone else for that matter. She was attracted to Rick, sure, but more than that, she liked being with him and talking with him. He made her laugh. He was even thoughtful when he wasn't provoking her into a display of temper.

She smiled against her knees, hugging them to her chest. Maybe she did owe them a chance. Maybe. Her smile faded. But she wasn't rushing into anything.

"Can I think about it and give you an answer in the

morning?'' she asked, her voice tentative. She studied him in the moonlight, wondering at the thoughts behind his shadowed features.

"Is it such a tough decision? My ego really needs to know."

She sighed. "For me it is."

"Because of the geek-hunting project."

"Yes." Her chin lifted. "It's not a perfect plan, but I think it's going to break my habit of falling for looks and charm."

He made a rude noise but didn't comment, the distance in his manner a palpable thing.

Masking her conflicted feelings, she turned her face toward the heavens, studying the pinpoints of light as they revolved like a kaleidoscope's view of the night sky. Silence reigned as the merry-go-round gradually slowed to a stop.

Rick spoke up quietly. "Well, it's getting late. Come on and I'll walk you up."

As they crossed the grassy field that separated the playground from their apartment building, Haley struggled to make a decision. She sensed that Rick was on the verge of giving up on her. If she turned him down now he wouldn't ask her out again. He'd move on and tonight's playful interlude would be the last of its kind. From this point on, they'd be nothing more than nodding acquaintances who just happened to live in side-by-side apartments.

Something inside of her rebelled against such an outcome. The internal battle all but lost and won, she quietly ascended the stairs at his side. At the top, she grabbed his elbow. "Wait."

Still holding the rail, he turned to face her, blue eyes dark and questioning.

"Maybe I don't need to think about it overnight—Oh!" This last was wrenched from her as a couple of teenagers rushed past them and down the steps. She felt herself teetering on the top step until Rick grabbed her elbow to steady her. Taking her hand, he led her down the hall and into the relative shelter of his doorway. There he turned to stare down at her, his eyes intense.

"You were saying?"

"I was saying I didn't need any more time to think about this. I—"

Her words broke off at sight of a note taped to Rick's door, and the splotch of red at the bottom of it. The splotch, when she peered closer, turned out to be a woman's lip prints, stamped in bright red lipstick like a signature and an invitation. The prints looked real.

Frowning, she plucked the note free and turned to read it. She'd gotten as far as "Dear Ricky" and "I'm lonely" before Rick snatched the paper out of her hands. He glanced at it then crumpled it up.

"Forget the note. It's nothing. Now tell me what you were going to say."

Haley considered him with a raised eyebrow. *So it's "nothing," huh? Gee, that sounds just a little too familiar.* Suddenly, she felt the bitter urge to kick someone. She just didn't know whether the target ought to be him for tempting her so badly or herself for ignoring everything her lousy ex-boyfriends ever taught her. "I was saying good-night, Rick. Thanks for the...diversion tonight. I enjoyed it for what it was worth." She smiled with her lips and glared with her eyes. "And thanks for the invitation, but the answer is no."

She ducked under his arm and stalked off to her apartment. *Casual.* She should have just kept everything casual and friendly, damn it. Would she never learn? How could she have forgotten, even for one moment, all of Rick's women? So many women after him. Surely not without some encouragement from him. Thank God for the reminder taped to his door, or she might have ruined everything and joined the lineup of women desperate for a crumb of attention.

As she was digging her keys out of her pocket, Rick grabbed her arm and turned her to face him. "I told you that note was nothing. I don't even know who the hell Franny is."

"Franny? Well, think back. Think bright red lipstick. Ring any bells?" She batted her eyelashes up at him and tugged free of his grip.

"Look, she's just another one of those women who—"

...*just another one of those women...* Haley's temper flared. "Oh, give it up. I've seen the women lining up at your door. And yes, I could see where you'd think this one meant nothing more than all the others. I've had boyfriends who thought something similar about me. Hell, I think I could even work up some sympathy for this Franny-who-means-nothing-to-you."

He spoke through gritted teeth. "I'll bet you could. Seems to me you have a lot in common with her. More than you know." He turned without another word and went back to his own door.

It was a strained silence as they both fumbled with

doorlocks. God, she knew she was overreacting, but this stupid, unfounded jealousy just stung so much. And she'd been such an idiot about Rick. Distance. She needed distance from the man. And perspective.

Haley managed to get her door open first—no doubt because of a recent application of WD-40, she mused grimly, feeling hurt and stupid and spiteful. Yeah, the man was just a jack of all trades. With women, locked doors, recalcitrant dogs.

She glared at him over her shoulder. "And stay away from my dog!" The door slammed behind her.

INSIDE, HALEY THREW HER KEYS onto the couch. When they fell between the cushions, she just snorted. Who cared if she had to find them later? She probably ought to be locked up for her own good anyway. Look how close she'd come to making another huge mistake. Thank heavens for guardian angels who protected fools and small children. That note was a lucky save.

So why didn't she feel lucky?

Her anger dissipated until only a dull ache remained. Slowly, she trudged up the stairs to the bedroom, where she greeted Sherlock briefly then tugged off her clothes. She slipped on a huge T-shirt that covered her to her knees. It was Football Flynn's old jersey, if she remembered correctly. And apparently she was in need of a good reminder about the perils of falling for men who were too good-looking for her own good, she scolded herself as she climbed into bed.

"SO, HOW DID THE BIG DATE GO?" Jen asked as the door closed behind an elderly customer.

Haley glanced at her friend, and then away. "Oh, not so good."

"Not quite what you expected?" Jen folded her arms across her chest, a satisfied look on her face.

Haley wrinkled her nose. "No, not really. I know I'm on the right track, though." She glanced away, her mouth tightening. "Nothing like a little negative reinforcement to build up the resolve again."

"Uh-oh. What happened?"

Grabbing her favorite stuffed hound, Haley plopped into a beanbag chair. She smoothed long, plush ears and stared into the dog's soulful eyes. "I spent some time with Rick after my date last night."

"This sounds interesting." Jen leaned against the counter. "Spill it."

At Jen's obvious interest, Haley wished she'd kept her mouth closed. "Well, first the date with Tim kind of fell flat. He's a nice guy, but—"

"But just nothing there? No spark? No connection?" At Haley's dejected shrug, Jen nodded knowingly. "Just let the 'I told you so' go unsaid, then, and get to the good stuff. What happened with Rick?"

Haley hugged the stuffed dog to her chest. "It was great at first. Silly and fun and romantic. He was even sweet...helped me clean up after Sherlock went on a rampage. But then..."

"Yes?"

Haley sighed and related the rest of the evening to Jen, ending with the note and Rick's arrogant dismissal of it.

"But—" Jen shook her head, obviously baffled. "Didn't he explain about the note?"

Haley half-growled. "Sure, he did. I'm to understand that this woman and her lip prints mean nothing to him. I'm supposed to accept her as just another faceless female in his crowd of admirers." She shook her head. "But I can't do that. I can't be just another in a long line of women. I'm not wired that way."

"Well, of course you're not. Why should you be?" Jen squeezed her arm bracingly.

Haley sighed. "You know, the hardest part about all this is that I'd actually started to believe Rick was different. That one woman—that *I* might be enough for him. That maybe I was special to him. Guess I was wrong."

"I just don't get it." Jen shook her head. "I really thought the guy liked you. That just sucks."

"No kidding."

"Oh, Haley." Jen draped an arm around her and hugged her tight. "I swear, sometimes men have all the sensitivity of an animal in heat. He's chasing you like there's no other woman in the world for him, while at the same time, he's got this other woman taping love notes to his door."

"And don't forget all the others." Haley grimaced. "Might as well have a revolving door to his apartment, considering all the women who've come knocking."

Jen scowled. "Men are dogs."

"Complete dogs."

"Well, all except Frank."

Haley's lips twitched reluctantly. "Yeah. Except Frank. Are you sharing, by any chance?"

Jen grinned back at her. "Not in this lifetime."

"Damn. Can't even count on my best friend." Haley

shook her head sorrowfully, trying to ignore the very real ache that still lingered deep in her heart.

Why couldn't Rick have been different?

"PETER."

Haley stared into the smoothly handsome face of her ex-boyfriend. He was standing at her door and smiling like nothing had changed between them. Mentally, she rolled her eyes at his obtuseness. Behind her, Sherlock barked incessantly, protesting an intruder on his territory.

"Hi, Haley." Dressed smartly in pressed slacks and a casual sport shirt, he leaned against the door frame and folded tan arms across his chest. "I said I'd be by for my tennis racquet, so..." Peter glanced beyond her into the apartment, his gaze expectant.

Suddenly, the idea of revenge didn't seem all that satisfying. She just wanted him gone. She sighed. "You should have tried calling again instead of just showing up uninvited. It was a wasted trip."

Peter frowned, confused. "But I'm sure I left my racquet here."

A nearby door swung open and Rick strode out. He gave Haley a blank stare, saw the man next to her, then broke into a wide, toothy smile. "Haley. How are you, sweetheart."

She stared, feeling a little stunned. Here was another man acting as though recent, unpleasant events had never occurred. What was it with men? The evening had taken a turn for the surreal.

Unfazed by her lack of response, Rick joined Haley and smiled a challenge at the man next to her. "Hi. I don't believe we've met. I'm Rick. A good friend of Haley's." Rick smoothly positioned himself between Haley and Peter, offering his hand.

Peter reluctantly accepted it. "Peter. Haley's boyfriend. Nice to meet you."

"*Ex*-boyfriend, Peter." Haley's words sliced neatly into the conversation.

"Wait, Haley. You never gave me a chance to explain. That business at the office was just...in the heat of the moment, you know? It wasn't quite the way it seemed."

"Really?" Haley just stared at Peter and felt utterly repelled by both him and her own lack of judgment. What a shallow slime. "So the sight of a man and woman naked and sucking each other's faces could be misconstrued? Silly me. So where's Trixie or Bambi or Bippy or whatever her name is?"

"Uh, Tawny. Her name's Tawny." Peter shifted uncomfortably, his cheekbones flushed. "But it was barely even a fling, I swear. I didn't even care when she started seeing some other guy. And now that I've had a chance to think...well..." He glanced at Rick, distracted. "Would you mind excusing us, uh, Rick? As you can see, we have some sensitive matters to discuss."

Feeling her temper spark at his presumption, Haley smiled wickedly. "Oh, that's all right, Peter. Rick knows the whole story. He won't be embarrassed if you're a little blunt. But it's a moot point anyway. We're through."

"Really, Haley. Can't we discuss all this calmly?" His teeth flashed in a smile she used to find endearing.

The spark caught fire. "No, Peter, I really don't think so. Go away."

"But what about my racquet?"

The flames leapt out of control. "You want your racquet? Fine." Slamming the door in their faces, she swung around to the laundry room and snatched up the hated object. Then, with appropriately feral fanfare, she yanked the door open and presented the mangled mass for Peter's horrified inspection. "Here."

Peter gingerly accepted the splintered wooden handle, grasping the misshapen head with his other, trembling hand. "My favorite racquet. Haley, how could you?"

"Oh, heat of the moment. You know how it is. Maybe Boopsie will help you shop for a new favorite racquet."

"Er...*Tawny*, but...?"

Ignoring her ex's sputtering, Haley turned a determined smile on Rick. "Now, if you don't mind, Peter, Rick and I have some sensitive matters to discuss—" She tugged Rick into the apartment and closed the door firmly in Peter's face.

Once the door was closed, Haley pressed her ear against it, listening for Peter's retreating footsteps. When the sounds receded, she turned and leaned back against the door, her gaze resting on the man who waited silently for her attention. She met Rick's twinkling gaze with a rueful smile of her own.

"So was revenge everything you'd hoped it would be?" Rick watched her as he absently petted Sherlock.

"Actually, it would have been a lot more satisfying if I wasn't reminded so strongly of my own stupidity. What kind of bad judgment would cause a reasonably intelligent woman to date a creep like that?" A memory of the previous night's events flashed through her mind. Her smile faded and she straightened.

Studying her, Rick gave Sherlock a last pat then slid thoughtfully onto the couch. "I guess it would be the same kind of bad judgment that would cause a woman to date a creep like *me*. So how come I'm on the inside and he's out in the cold?"

Her gaze slid away from his. "Because it was convenient. And your offense was less."

"Ah. We begin to see the light. Yes, it was. Much less, in fact. I still don't know who Franny is."

"Just a secret admirer, I guess?" She eyed him doubtfully.

"Kind of. There are some desperately lonely people out there, Haley."

"Like me?"

His smile was gentle. "No, not like you. You want a future with a decent guy. That's understandable. However, I don't see you stalking a stranger and leaving a suggestive note with your lipstick smeared across the bottom of it."

"No, I guess not." She studied him a moment. "So, Franny was a complete stranger?"

"Honest. I swear it on my best dirt bike. I have no idea who that woman was and if I ever came face to face with her I'd probably take off running. Her kind terrify me."

Haley laughed, partially relieved. *A stranger, not "nothing."* It didn't explain away the other women or give her permission to go out with him...but at least he wasn't another Peter who could just dismiss women he dated as nothing.

"So, does that mean we're friends again?"

She sighed. "Sure. Friends."

He patted the cushion next to him. "So sit."

She slumped next to him, and rested her chin on her chest. After a moment, she shook her head, a humorless smile sliding across her lips. "I feel like such an idiot. Peter's so obviously a jerk. Why didn't I see it before?"

"You're not an idiot. I'd say you're an optimist." He smiled. "And maybe a bit of a romantic, despite that smart mouth of yours."

She rested her head on the back of the couch. "Make that a woman who left her brain behind and followed a foolish, fickle heart."

"Oh, I don't think you give your heart enough credit."

She rolled her head to look at him. "What do you mean?"

"I don't think your heart bought into that guy. You don't seem devastated by your breakup. My guess is your pride took a nasty beating and the heart only got bruised a little."

She closed her eyes, considering his words. "You know, Jen said the same thing. You're probably right." She opened her eyes and smiled ruefully at him. "So, is that good news or bad news?"

He reached over and brushed a stray lock of hair away from her eyes. A smile bloomed on his lips, sexy and slow. "Good news. Real good news."

Her breathing hitched and grew shallow but she couldn't look away. And she couldn't move away. Fascinated, she watched his curving lips, masculine and firm, yet so sensual and oh, so tempting as they drew closer and closer. She inhaled sharply, tasting the moist warmth of his breath, and waited. But he touched only the barest kiss to her mouth before easing back.

Glancing up into his eyes, she lifted a hand to his cheek, lingering over its sandpaper texture. His eyes slitted as he leaned into her caress. With a low cry, she slid her hand to the back of his head and tugged him close, tunneling her fingers deeply into the shaggy blond silk of his hair.

He slanted his head and took her mouth hungrily, lips and tongue exploring and taking, as he locked strong arms around her waist and hips.

Absorbing the heat of his passion, she eagerly sought more, molding herself against his chest. She wrapped her arms around his neck and held on tight. He felt so good, hard as a rock. Like she could tumble across him without unsettling him. She could climb right into his arms and stay there, immersing herself in his passion and his humor and his sweetness until she was senseless with it.

*Senseless with it…*again.

Groaning, Haley shoved away from him. For a moment, he held tightly to her, as though refusing to let her go. Then, reluctantly, he loosened his hold.

Trembling, she sat back, her eyes wide. He studied her, his gaze fiery. She couldn't stop staring at him. Every hormonal inch of her wanted nothing more than to fall back into his arms and let this keening ache overrule her common sense.

He moved as if to reclaim her, when she launched off the couch. She moved several paces away, avoiding his eyes as she tried to steady herself.

"Oh, boy." She inhaled. "That shouldn't have happened. Really, really shouldn't have happened." Oh, God, but she'd wanted it to. She wished it could have happened. Not now, but before she'd sworn off hunks and charmers, when she could have allowed herself to indulge in this madness. She glared at him over her shoulder. "Why couldn't you have showed up in my life a year ago?" She huffed and paced, using anger to burn away some of this awful frustration. "Typical male timing."

"Why a year ago?" His voice was a rich, husky sound that raised the hair on the back of her neck. "Is that when you decided geeks were the way to go?"

"That's when I met Peter."

He rolled to his feet in one lithe movement, approaching her slowly, steadily. "You wouldn't have dated Peter if I'd seen you first."

She batted away the hand he touched to her shoulder. Still the sparks shot to her belly and lower. "Of course I wouldn't have. That's my point. You could have been my last fling before I got serious about finding someone."

He wrapped long hard fingers around her arm and turned her to face him. His eyes narrowed. "I would have been a 'last fling'?"

Her gaze caressed his sexy mouth, the strong lines of his face, the mouthwatering shoulders and chest and— She yanked her thoughts off that dangerous path, inhaled, sighed. "Oh, yeah." She closed her eyes, almost in pain. "But it's too late now. I'm through playing with men. It's time to get serious about all this." She raised her chin, eyeing him resolutely. "So we need to just forget about what happened."

His gaze still hot, Rick shook his head slowly. "I don't think we can do that. I want you so bad I can taste it. I think you want me just as much."

"Of course I do. And that's why I can't trust my judgment where you're concerned. So keep your distance."

A harsh sound echoed deep in his throat. "You're nuts."

"No doubt." She smiled wistfully at him. "And right now I need to be alone. So get out."

"I'm not going anywhere until we get this straightened out."

Her smile faded. "I guess this isn't going to work, then. I thought we could at least remain friends, but if you can't just forget what happened here, maybe we should keep our distance." She swallowed past the lump in her throat but kept her gaze steady on his.

"No." The word burst from him and he reached out a hand. Slowly, he withdrew it. "I mean, let's not blow this out of proportion." Stepping back a pace, he raked a hand through his hair, and exhaled deeply. Then he turned a version of his old, cocky grin on her. "It was just a kiss, right?"

She eyed him uncertainly. "Right."

"Okay. So, you want us to be friends. Nothing more."

"Yes." She watched him, trying to read his thoughts. "That means we date other people, not each other."

His brow lowered. "You mean you're still going through with your plan."

She nodded silently, ignoring an ache deep in her belly. *Lord, but this was hard.* "And that means I don't want you to see me as some kind of challenge or something you need to conquer. We're friends. Period."

His eyes narrowed. "I wouldn't pursue you just for the challenge of it, Haley. Men left the cave a long time ago."

His uncompromising tone shamed her a little. "Right. You're right. I'm sorry." She shrugged awkwardly. "Like I tried to tell you, I'm a really bad judge of character when it comes to dating and men."

He stared a moment longer. "So why don't you let me help you find a guy?"

Poor Rick. He apparently had just suffered a brain malfunction. *"What?"*

"If you don't trust your own judgment, why don't you let me help you decide which guys to date?" He spoke the words slowly, as though still testing out an idea.

He was going to help her find another man? Unbelievable. Feeling equal parts amazement and hurt, she just sputtered for a moment. "You're the one who's nuts." Just moments ago, he'd wanted her for himself. Now he was offering to find another guy to take his place. That, more than anything, should tell her how shallow his feelings for her ran. She was right to set aside this crazy attraction.

"No, I'm serious." He held out a hand to her. "Look, if we're friends, then I'm only going to want the best for you. Right?"

Ignoring his hand, she stared at him, speechless.

"Right," he responded for her, dropping his hand. "So it's settled. I'll screen your geeks for you."

6

BACK IN HIS APARTMENT, Rick yanked his shirt over his head, his frustration eating him alive. He'd been right to back off, but damn, it had taken everything he had to let her go, even temporarily. It wasn't so much that she'd said no to sex. He wasn't a teenager, and he could control his urges when the situation called for it.

No, what really bugged him was the way she still refused to trust him. Sure, after he'd calmed down last night, he'd understood how that note on his door could have upset Haley. It was pretty incriminating. But now, even after he'd explained the note to her satisfaction, the woman continued to be stubborn and blind. Couldn't she see the potential sizzling between them?

No, she couldn't see beyond his face and what she considered a dead-end job at a bike shop. She figured him for a good-looking jock with no sense of honor or compassion. And he had this sinking feeling that she took every word he said with a grain of salt. It made him nuts.

Sure, he could probably win her over if he told her everything. She was attracted to him and seemed to enjoy being with him. Finding out how much he had in common with her geeky prospects would probably override her reservations.

He sighed, reflecting. He'd only told her about the

bike shop, which for him qualified more as a hobby than a real moneymaker like Computer Nation. Owning the chain of successful computer stores made him eligible even in town celebrities' eyes. But he'd deliberately kept that bit of information from her, first because she was female and might have heard about his recent notoriety, and then later because of his own contrariness.

Maybe it was stupid, but he just couldn't cave to her reverse snobbery and tell her the whole truth. It was the principle of the thing. So he continued to let her believe that his ambitions amounted to nothing more than a throwaway bike shop job.

Now it looked as though she assumed he was playing at life with no thought for the future. She seemed to see him as an overgrown, penniless jock with a constant stream of women passing through his life. If she only knew.

Still, if he told her everything now and won her over that way, she'd just be dating him for his computer expertise, his socially awkward past and, quite possibly, his bank account.

Maybe she didn't want the money or prestige. Call him crazy, but he'd rather she date him *in spite of* what he did for a living, not because of it. And, frankly, those were his only two choices at the moment, because for her, occupation seemed to say more about a man than it should.

Besides, he was sick and tired of women making snap judgments about him based on his looks or wealth. He didn't like being pegged and he damn sure didn't like being used.

No, Haley wasn't malicious or a gold-digger as he'd first assumed. She was, however, just begging for a lesson against stereotyping people. And he knew just how to do it.

First things first, though. He had to stall for a little time. He'd need his cousin's help to open Haley's eyes, and Greg wasn't due in town for a while yet.

"YOU'RE SURE ABOUT THIS?" Haley glanced around doubtfully. The tiny shop was neatly packed with shelves full of model kits, train set components, balsa wood in every shape and thickness, paints, odd tools and enough fume-producing glue to daze an entire population.

Dazed. Did she want a glue-dazed man? She slid a narrow glance at Rick. "A hobby shop? Really?"

"Trust me. I'm your geek screener. Would I steer you wrong?"

She raised an eyebrow. "In a heartbeat. Now keep your voice down, if you don't mind."

He grinned. "Hey, I was just offering a last warning to the observant."

She rolled her eyes and resolved to ignore him. Scanning the aisles, she immediately discarded two young males who were looking a little too interested in the glue section. For the sake of caution, she even skipped over the guy intent on wicked-looking spray paint. Glancing around, she settled on a slender man—about her age, thank heavens—who was gazing into a glass display case filled with...stamps? Postage stamps. A stamp collector.

She smiled, touched. That was sweet. Traditional.

Normal. And postage sounded so darned...*reliable*.
Perfect. Things were definitely looking up. As casually
as she was able, Haley strolled down the aisle toward
the glass case.

Watching her and forcing himself to hang back
slightly, Rick felt his own good humor shriveling up
and hardening. Hell. It wasn't supposed to work like
this. She was supposed to walk in here, see a bunch of
retirees and adolescents, maybe a Tim-alike or two,
then turn away and leave. A lesson. A demonstration.

Not a fresh opportunity, damn it. Did the woman
never give up?

I GIVE UP, Haley silently mourned. Her plan was not
working. Stamp collecting. Sure it was reliable. Sure it
was...traditional.

"...and thith one here ith even more valuable be-
cauth it..." Jared the stamp collector droned pleasantly
on, his smile benign, his eyes gently appreciative as he
studied the display.

The man had a lisp. *And he lived with hith mother. Who
enjoyed thtamp collecting ath much ath her thon did.*

Haley could only assume the man had licked one too
many *thtampth*. Could a woman get used to something
like a lisp in the man she loved? Haley blinked, feeling
disappointment well deep in her belly. Sure she could.
If she really loved the man. Or if she felt anything at all
for the man other than the mild kindness one would
experience toward one of nature's more harmless creatures.

She smiled regretfully, opened her mouth to make
discreet excuses before leaving—

"Hi, babe. You about ready to go?" Rick slipped an arm around her waist, gave it an intimate squeeze, and glanced at the clock. "That fertility specialist is not gonna be happy if we're late for our appointment."

Haley goggled. "Wha—?"

"Well, shoot." Rick flashed an apologetic smile at Jared, whose cheeks were flushing a blotchy red. "Haley insisted on the best, so we got the best, but the doc's always booked." He turned a patiently affectionate glance on Haley. "And, no offense, honey, but you're only going to ovulate for so long."

"Fertil— Ovu—" Haley was certain her tongue had swollen to three times its normal size; she couldn't seem to get a word out.

Rick shrugged, supremely fatalistic. "Hell, one week, tops, and that egg's history. Time to get hatching." So saying, he swept Haley around and steered her toward the door.

"It wath nith meeting you." Jared spoke up politely. "And, er, good luck?"

When Haley and Rick emerged from the store, Rick's shoulders were already shaking with mirth.

Haley was shaking for an entirely different reason. "You. Are. Certifiable."

"I know. Completely nuts." Rick gave her a cajoling grin and a one-armed hug. "But I did come to your rescue."

She jerked away and marched over to his car, wishing with all her might that she'd had the wisdom to drive separately. "Rescue, ha. Like I needed rescuing by you. And you are *so* fired. No more screening my dates for me. I couldn't handle the humiliation."

"Now, Haley." With obvious effort, Rick tried to smother the huge grin on his face.

"Now, Haley, nothing. Fertility specialist? What were you *thinking?* I thought poor Jared would have a coronary on the spot."

"Not to mention your reaction. The look on your face was just priceless." Rick snorted with amusement, glanced at her again, and covered his chuckles by clearing his throat. "Sorry." *Cough.* "Frog in my throat." He pounded his chest for effect, but his eyes still sparkled with laughter.

Haley closed her eyes, feeling her face burn, even as she fought back a grin herself. It had been funny. Jared had been almost purple, his eyes wide and blinking rapidly. She turned aside so Rick couldn't see her face, and silently climbed into the car.

After rounding to the driver's side, Rick dropped into his seat and started the ignition.

When Haley still didn't speak, Rick glanced over. "Oh, come on, Haley. I know you didn't really like the guy. It was written all over your face in there. So, it's for the best. I mean, at least this way the guy's thinking he's well rid of us—lunatics that we are—instead of pining after you for a decade or two. Right?"

Haley's lips quivered. "A decade or two? I think I deserve an eternity at least." She pressed her lips straight.

"Hell, if that's what it takes, *I'll* pine after you for an eternity." He gave her a ridiculously soulful look that lost her the battle.

Surrendering to a twisted grin, she closed her eyes

and shook her head. "You're still a nutcase. *Fertility specialist?*"

"Hey, it's all I could think of, and you needed rescuing, whether you knew it or not."

She sighed. "Maybe." *How depressing.*

"That's better." He put the car in gear and pulled out. "So are you ready for the next leg of the hunt?" He gave her a sunny smile.

She winced. *"Must* you call it that?"

TWO HOURS LATER HALEY stalked into The Toy Boxx, a twitchy-lipped Rick right behind her. Jen glanced up curiously, eyes taking on a cautious glint as she noted the promise of warfare in Haley's expression.

"Hello." Jen glanced back and forth between them. "I guess things didn't go quite as planned?"

"You could say that." Haley tilted her chin mutinously. "Any problems this morning?"

"Nope. Just expecting heavier traffic for the afternoon shift. And here you are to help."

Haley nodded, ignoring Rick.

"Hey, wait up, Hale."

She glanced back at him furiously. "If you're wise, you'll keep your mouth closed and just do your penance. Boxes. In the back."

Rick rolled his eyes. In a pitying moment he'd actually promised to help Haley unload some new freight. Right after failed geek encounter number four? Five? He wasn't sure. Things kind of blurred together after Fred from the copy shop waxed poetic on the virtues of quality paper and skilled photocopying. Rick had felt it necessary to verbally weigh the cash outlay for copy-

ing versus just printing the blasted document out on a
home printer. Fred had been a little miffed. Haley even
more so.

Or maybe he'd agreed to penance after the library
incident, when he'd burst the bubble of some college
professor on the make. Hey, it wasn't his fault if, in an
attempt to be helpful to the guy and look up a refer-
ence location or two on the computer, Rick had bun-
gled the Dewey decimal system and mistakenly wan-
dered into a section dealing with male impotence. Or
that the guy had felt defensive enough to take it personally. Okay, so maybe some of it had been inten-
tional, but still—

"Wait just a minute, all right?" In one quick stride,
Rick managed to snag Haley's elbow. "Maybe it wasn't
all pleasant, but I think we made progress. I'm here to
screen your dates for you, not okay all the wrong guys.
And that's what I did. Helped you eliminate some of
the negatives. Right?" He tried for a supremely reasonable look.

Haley looked supremely pissed. "You're supposed
to help me find a guy, not shoot down every one of my
prospects." Yanking her elbow free, she stalked off to
the supply room, ignoring the knowing grin Jen
flashed at her.

Jen didn't have to say a word. After Haley had for-
mally introduced Jen to Rick when he'd picked her up
for the hobby shop expedition, the two had hit it off.
They were united in wholehearted agreement on the
stupidity of Haley's plan and felt no qualms about telling her so.

In fact, Haley was outnumbered completely. Jen had

cheered for Rick all along and their instant camaraderie this morning seemed to have cemented her high opinion of him—if her smug looks were any indication. Problem was, Haley was finding it annoyingly difficult to disagree with Jen. Rick was handsome and funny and sweet. Oh, the absolute *gall* of the man to be so damn perfect when she couldn't keep him for herself.

He'd even worked wonders with the dog from Hades. Under Rick's excellent tutelage, Sherlock was learning to respond to any number of commands. Too bad he only responded to *Rick's* voice. He'd explained, with thinly concealed amusement, that a man's deeper voice naturally carried more authority than a woman's. Given time and practice, Sherlock would learn to obey her as well.

Maybe given time and practice, *Rick* would learn to respond to her commands, too. At least regarding her love life. Never had a man offered so much help and yet found so many ways to obstruct a simple goal.

Rick, who'd followed Haley to the stock room, halted in front of the large box she silently indicated. He bent to lift it. "Holy—" He grunted the rest as he hefted the surprisingly weighty box onto his shoulder. "What's in this thing? A load of rocks?"

She led him out to the sales floor and showed him where to set the box. He eyed her suspiciously but did as she requested. Haley opened the box. Speechless, he gaped at the plastic bags inside...each one filled with polished stones.

Obviously listening in on their exchange, Jen started laughing. Rick shot her a wry look before returning his attention to the tiny spitfire who was becoming almost an obsession for him.

"Funny, Haley. Look. I couldn't, in good conscience, let you date any of these guys. None of them is a match for you. You'd walk all over every one of them. Not to mention that you'd be bored to tears because you have nothing in common."

"So Fred was a little...wrong for me. I can understand that. But what exactly did you have against Professor Thomas? And what about poor Jared? I might have grown to like him over time. He seemed decent enough."

Rick rolled his eyes. "The fact that you can call a grown man 'poor' anything should be explanation enough. You would have sliced and diced any one of these guys the first time you had a disagreement. Professor Thomas obviously has some serious...*hang-ups* of his own to deal with. And your poor Jared needs to find himself a quiet, unassuming woman who likes stamp collecting as much as he and his mother do."

Stubbornly squelching her own agreement with his conclusions, she stared accusingly at him. "Well, the hobby shop was your idea. Why did you suggest it anyway? You're the one who's so against me looking for a decent geek to date. So tell me. Why did we go to all these supposed hangouts anyway?"

Because I don't want you to find some loveable, average Joe to take my place. Rick squelched the tiny, disturbing little voice and deliberately replaced it with another. *Because I need you single and still looking when Greg gets here.* Aloud, he explained, "Hobby shops and libraries are good places to find men with goals and interests other than sports, TV and bar-hopping. Isn't that part of what you're looking for in a husband?"

"I guess so." Still, she frowned at him suspiciously.

He flashed his best winning smile.

Her eyes narrowed and she studied him silently for a moment. Then a slow, crafty grin tugged at her mouth.

He braced himself.

"I have an idea."

"That's what scares me. Okay, go on."

"Since you don't approve of any of the prospects I've selected, why don't *you* find a decent guy for me to date?"

His eyes widened. "Now, wait a minute. My job is to screen the guys *you* pick out, not find them for you."

Her smile widened. "It shouldn't be too much of a problem for you. Don't you have some friends you can set me up with? Some commitment-friendly, serious-minded friends?"

Relief washed over him. "Nope. Not a one. They're all shallow, womanizing, chauvinistic pigs. Not a marriage prospect in the bunch."

"No big surprise there. You know what they say about the company a man keeps."

Bullet hole through the instep. Damn it. "Just kidding. I'll see what I can do."

"JEN, ARE YOU SURE THIS GUNK works?" The phone pressed to her ear, Haley surveyed the two bowls in front of her.

Jen laughed. "I know, it sounds disgusting. But I found the recipes in a magazine a few years ago. You know, one of those articles claiming there's no need to buy the expensive stuff when you can make something cheap and similar at home? Anyway, this regimen works for me. I swear by it. Now put the phone down and give it a try."

"You're sure this isn't some whacked-out revenge plan?" Haley frowned warily. "I already apologized for leaving you alone with the demon child this afternoon. Next time you can make the deposit while I deal with the difficult customers. Deal?"

Haley wrinkled her nose at the thought of dealing with the spoiled customer by herself. It wasn't a pleasant idea. She knew the child's real name was Johnny, but they'd privately nicknamed him the demon child because he had a big allowance and no manners or respect.

"Not nearly good enough, sweetie. That child is a tyrant. You owe me. I think you get to close next Saturday night. Then we'll be even."

"*Or* how about I don't strangle you for encouraging Rick to sabotage my love life?" Haley's voice rose pointedly.

"Okay, deal." Jen laughed and hung up.

Haley set the receiver down and eyed the green mess in bowl number one. "Okay, first things first." She pulled her hair back and secured it with a terry cloth headband, thought a minute, then tugged it off again. "Why don't I just do it all at once and get the mess over with? Great plan, Hale."

Nodding in resolution, Haley scooped up some of the green gunk and smeared it over her face, paying special attention to the all-important T-zone as Jen had suggested. *Ugh. This better be worth it.* She'd better have men writing sonnets to her radiant complexion and shiny hair by this time tomorrow, or Jen was going to pay.

Once she had a thick layer of green gunk smeared evenly over her face, Haley rinsed her hands and turned to the shiny white glob in the other bowl. Mostly mayonnaise, so it couldn't be that bad. Okay. Scooping it up, she bent her head over the kitchen sink—the kitchen had seemed most appropriate, given the ingredients—and worked the concoction into her dampened hair.

Finished, she wrapped a towel around her hair then dumped the bowls into the sink. While she was giving the mass an extra twist for security, she heard a familiar, whimpering bark from behind.

"No, Sherlock, wait. Go outside? Go potty outside?" Haley spoke in an excited, high-pitched voice. The idea was to distract the puppy from his squatting inclinations long enough for them to find a nice grassy spot outside. Somehow she had a feeling Sherlock would *never* puddle on *Rick's* floor. *Hers*, on the other hand, was still fair game.

She ran for the leash and snapped it onto his collar. Then she dragged the hunched-over animal out the door and down the steps, trying not to notice the wet trail following them.

"Come on, Sherlock. That's a good boy. Almost there—wait!"

The puppy squirmed free of his new collar and bounded toward the hedge of bushes lining the side-walk. Haley took off after him, ignoring the towel that came loose of her makeshift turban. She grimaced as slimy locks of hair slid free to cling to her neck and shoulders.

Lunging, she managed to snag a hind paw as the dog tried to wiggle through the shrubbery. The pup yelped and twisted, throwing her off balance. She landed on all fours and was scrambling for better footing when she heard voices approaching. Thinking of the gunk smeared over her face and matting her hair, Haley shimmied through the bushes to kneel beneath their cover next to Sherlock.

"Oh, Rick, honey. You have such a wonderful sense of humor. I just love getting together with you like this." The breathy voice trailed off suggestively.

Haley rolled her eyes but strained to hear Rick's response as she refastened Sherlock's collar and leash.

"It was good seeing you again, Selina, but like I said— Mmmph!"

Frowning, Haley peered through the greenery at the tall, curvy blonde who looked to be massaging Rick's tonsils. With her tongue. White-hot jealousy shot through her, and she had to suppress the overwhelming desire to yank on the blonde's tongue until her ears flapped against her head. Gritting her teeth, Haley reminded herself that Rick was only doing what she'd suggested; he was dating other women. They had absolutely no claim on each other.

The blonde wrapped a long leg around Rick's hips.

"Oh, spare me," Haley muttered to Sherlock.

The dog barked his agreement. Haley wrapped a hand around his muzzle, but it was too late.

Rick tore himself free of the woman's greedy lips,

dodging that mouth as it attempted a foray along his neck. "No, wait, Selina. That dog sounded like my neighbor's."

Sherlock whined beneath his restraint, and Rick broke away from the clinging woman to investigate. Haley squeezed her eyes shut and faced the inevitable.

She stood up slowly, grasping the dog's leash with one hand. Dreading the next few minutes, she opened her eyes.

Breathy Voice squealed. It was a dainty, sex kitten noise, Haley observed, feeling a little catty herself.

Rick's eyes widened in shock, his lips quirked, quivered, and then he surrendered to it. Knee-smacking, thigh-slapping, rip-roaring laughter. He laughed so hard and unrestrainedly that Haley wanted to do some smacking, slapping and rip-roaring of her own. Even Breathy Voice looked disconcerted at his display.

"Are you finished?" Haley asked in an icy voice. "My dog and I would like to return to our apartment."

Nose in the air and leash firmly in hand, Haley marched past the taller woman, who stepped back hastily with a grimace, then glided up the stairs with as much grace as she could manage. Once her apartment door was shut, Haley slumped against it, sliding all the way to the floor.

"This is all your fault, you know." Haley gazed sternly at her oversize puppy. Tail wagging, the dog clambered over her legs and began licking the avocado and cucumber concoction from her face. Ugh. She *so* needed a shower.

Half an hour later, free of homemade beauty concoctions and dressed in comfy, ugly clothes, Haley plopped down on her couch and aimed the remote at her TV. Just as she flipped to a promising sitcom, there was a knock at the door. Sighing, she clicked the TV off and went to answer the summons.

When she saw Rick's grinning face, she tried to slam the door closed again, but he blocked it with the flat of his hand. "Temper, temper."

She just glared.

"Come on, Haley. You have to admit you looked hilarious. Didn't you look in the mirror before you left your apartment?"

Haley grumbled and turned her back to him without closing the door.

Apparently considering it an invitation to enter, Rick did so and shut the door behind him. He plopped down on the couch next to where Haley had been sitting.

Still not ready to forgive him for her loss of dignity, Haley sat at the far end of the couch, shooting him dark looks from beneath her lashes.

Rick just waited, his eyes dancing with humor but not unkindly so. After a moment, Haley's lips twitched. He grinned at her and she threw a pillow at him, but she was laughing now. She must have been quite a sight, all green-faced with slimy Medusa locks dripping down her back. "It was all in the name of beauty, I'll have you know," she sputtered between giggles.

"Oh, I could tell."

"You rat. There I was looking all gunky and squatting in the shrubbery. And there you were, chortling like a fool. And you had to have your little—" She stopped laughing, glanced at him, then continued more cautiously. "—your *date* with you. So I had both of you for an audience. I suppose she thinks you have weirdos in your apartment building now."

He cocked his head, studying her with interest. "Does it matter what she thinks?"

Haley shrugged and looked away. "Is she your new girlfriend?" she asked casually.

"And if she were?"

She raised her chin and looked down her nose at him. "Then I'd ask if she knew exactly where you were right now, alone in an apartment with another woman. Think she'd stand for that?"

He smiled innocently. "Why should she mind? You're just my next-door neighbor. Perfectly innocent. Right?"

She glanced away. "Sure. So maybe you ought to introduce us next time."

Cupping her chin in one big hand, he tilted it until she was forced to meet his eyes. "I would, but she's not my girlfriend. Just someone I once dated. Very casually. I ran into her again today and she—" He shrugged uncomfortably. "She just sort of came with me. I couldn't get rid of her."

Haley rolled her eyes. "And you struggled so desperately to get away from her, too. What a sad little life you lead, with all these beautiful women throwing themselves violently at poor, helpless little you. God, I'm so glad I never got involved with you. To think—"

"Well, how's a guy *supposed* to fend off a woman who latches on to him like that?" He shifted uncomfortably. "A woman can always scream sexual harassment to get rid of a guy. But if a guy tries to give *her* the brush-off she gets weepy or insulted. Maybe even causes a scene or starts questioning his, um, orientation. Loudly. The guy ends up looking like a jerk no matter what he does."

Studying him, Haley realized he was being completely sincere. "So how did you get rid of her?"

He grinned sheepishly. "I told her you were a weirdo. Undergoing intense therapy for an odd personality disorder that causes you to go out dressed inappropriately. And seeing as you were a daughter of a friend of mine, I needed to look in on you and make sure you were okay."

Her eyes widened in disbelief.

He shrugged. "I was desperate." The grin widened. "And she believed me, too."

She scowled at him. "She'd probably believe you if you said the moon were made of blue cheese."

"No, but she'd believe me if I told her you liked to smear blue cheese salad dressing all over your face when you were feeling insecure."

He dodged the pillow she aimed at his laughing face and wrapped his arms around her to tackle her. Blocking her kicking feet and swatting hands, Rick easily subdued her beneath his weight.

Breathless from her struggles and reluctant laughter, she tried to repel him with menacing looks. The expression on his face told her she wasn't succeeding. He had her pinned, one big hand manacling her wrists above her head, his hard torso and thighs squashing her pleasantly beneath him. It was an undignified position. Pride alone should have overruled any sexual interest on her part.

Wistfully, Haley realized that pride alone didn't stand a chance against her response to this man. He laughed at her, made her laugh at herself, worked magic with her dog and was so hot she could just die. How fair was it that he tempt her like this?

Rick just grinned down at her, waiting.

Briefly, she considered renewing her struggles but rejected the idea almost immediately. The man had almost a hundred pounds on her, and muscles on top of muscles. Hard and warm and strong. Oh, boy.

Some of the longing must have shown on her face, because his expression changed. The gleam in his eyes grew darker, the grin more sensual, his grasp on her hands subtly more intimate. Her eyes widened.

"Something wrong, Hale?" The question came out in a husky whisper.

She just stared at the sexy curve of his lips, waiting and, heaven help her, *hoping.*

But he just shook his head. "Your move, honey."

"My?" She could barely speak around the thickness of her tongue.

He just nodded. She could feel the heat of his body, matched by his gaze.

Dumbly, feeling lost in the blue flames of his eyes, she nodded back, following the motion of his head for a moment. Then reason returned and she forced the nod into a negative shake. A violent one. "Get off me, you—you—"

"'You' what?" But he got off, slowly, letting her

know he could have remained if he'd chosen but was gentleman enough to obey her wishes.

"You did that on purpose." Her stare was accusing.

He shrugged, his eyes dancing as he watched her pace the room. "What if I did?"

"That's a violation of our deal. Remember? We're friends. That means no making moves on me."

"And I didn't, did I?"

She stopped pacing and jammed her fists on her hips. "You violated the spirit of the rules."

His eyebrows rose. "The 'spirit' of the rules? Man, you're tough."

She folded her arms across her chest and eyed him loftily. "Maybe I'm just a little more discriminating than your girlfriends."

He moved closer. "You were jealous. Admit it."

"I'll admit that I don't approve of your taste in women. Selina the siren was just a little obvious, don't you think?"

Rick grinned hugely. "I think you're so jealous it's killing you."

She raised her chin and stared down her nose at him—or as well as she could given the difference in their height. "I just hate to see a reasonably intelligent man letting his libido rule his social life."

"Why do women always underestimate the importance of a healthy, well-fed libido?" He watched her, a look of true enjoyment on his face.

"We don't underestimate it. We just don't let it take over completely. Show some restraint, for heaven's sake."

"Okay, since you seem to have it all figured out, tell

me what I ought to be looking for in a female companion."

Haley rose to the challenge. "Well, for starters, it would be nice if you had something in common with a woman, something to talk about or do together. You can't spend all your time in bed with her."

He looked wistful. "You don't think so?"

She shot him a look.

He laughed. "Okay, Haley. Since I seem to be doing it all wrong, why don't you help me find what you consider the perfect woman?"

She stepped back a pace, her eyes wide. "Help you find a woman?"

He smiled at her, an evil smile. "Sure. Consider it a fair trade. I help you find the right guy and you help me find the right woman. Deal?"

Haley considered his suggestion uneasily. Did she really want to help him find a woman who could enjoy him in a way she herself could not? *No.* But did she need to? *Probably.*

She sighed inwardly. If she went with her gut feeling, she'd say Rick was playing it straight with her, that he wanted to date her, and these other women meant nothing to him. But she'd been wrong so many times in the past. She couldn't trust herself, especially around a man like Rick, who had the uncanny ability to render her senseless when he got too close.

No, a smart woman would jump at the opportunity to eliminate temptation. Finding Rick a girlfriend would put him out of circulation and out of her reach. After all, she wouldn't poach on another woman's territory, so Rick would be more than off-limits.

Taking a deep breath, she nodded and stuck out a hand. "Deal. I find you a woman and you find me a man."

Rick shook on it, his grip warm and his smile challenging.

Withdrawing her hand and ignoring his smile, she moved purposefully toward her desk. She opened a drawer and extracted a familiar clipboard. As she walked back to the couch, she whipped the first few pages back until she found a blank page. She plopped down, curled her legs under her and waited while he approached more slowly.

"No time like the present." Her smile was determined. "Tell me what you're looking for in a woman."

He eyed the clipboard distrustfully. "Are you making another list?"

"Yes. Unless you have a better idea?"

His gaze rose to meet hers. "No, I suppose not."

"Okay. Fire away. Let's start with physical attributes."

He grinned. "This part I can handle.

She gave him a dirty look. "Let's keep it PG."

"Just when things start to get interesting— Okay, okay. Um, I like tall women. But short ones are a fun armful, too, so I guess height is negotiable. Long hair is nice. Not necessary, but nice."

Haley nodded, scribbling away. "Keep going."

He shifted on the couch. "I like a woman who's built. You know, big—"

"Yeah, yeah, I know. Selina proportions, right?"

His grin said it all. "Sure."

She slapped the clipboard down on her lap. "So why don't you date the siren if she's so perfect?"

He looked away, his eyes distant. "She isn't perfect, honey. Not by a long shot."

Haley's annoyance faded, and she studied him curiously. "She has the proportions right. So what's wrong with her?"

"I was kidding about the proportions, mostly to get a rise out of you." He grinned briefly, but his expression evened out to a more serious one that held secrets. "Let's just say she's not really interested in me."

"She only had her hands and lips all over you. How much more interested does she have to be?"

He pushed off the couch and went to look out the window at the playground below. Smiling slightly, he glanced over his shoulder at her. "Let's just say I can't see her whirling around on a merry-go-round with me."

Confused, Haley glanced down at her clipboard. She cleared her throat. "Personality differences. Okay. So, let's move on to personality."

"Hmm. How about genuine and fun-loving?"

Haley glanced up, surprised, but he'd already turned back to the window. When she spoke, her voice was soft, almost a whisper. "Those are good qualities. What else?"

"It would be nice to have a woman who didn't mind if her hair was a little messed up or her makeup wasn't caked on perfectly."

She nodded. "Okay. What about hobbies, interests?"

He shrugged and turned back to face her, leaning against the window frame with one shoulder. "I like biking. Computers. Amusement parks. Slapstick movies. It wouldn't hurt if she liked some of those things or at least didn't hate them."

Her fingers fumbling just a bit, Haley noted those details as well. Good Lord, if she hadn't seen all the other women chasing him, didn't already know how good-looking he was, how charming and sexy he could be, she'd almost think he was a caring, sensitive—

The clipboard was snatched out of her hands and Rick sat next to her. "Let's see what you've got here. Hmm...okay...okay. Yep, that about covers it." He looked up expectantly. "Your turn. Same order. Let's start with the 'physical attributes.'"

Haley crossed her arms over her chest, her eyes narrowed suspiciously. Here was the teasing playboy she knew Rick to be. "I'm suddenly having second thoughts."

"No fair. We shook hands on it. And we never did get to this part when I originally agreed to vet your geeks for you. It might help me to know some of this stuff. So give. What do you like in a guy?"

"Women aren't as picky about the physical stuff as men are." She held her head high, righteousness emanating from every pore.

He nodded wisely, scratching something on the paper.

She plucked the clipboard out of his hands and read it. "*Uptight?* You think I'm uptight? How do you get that from what I just said? I'm not uptight. Besides, we're not discussing me."

He grabbed the clipboard back and jotted something else down, his lips twitching.

She strained to read it also. "And now I'm *high maintenance?* Just because I object to being called uptight?"

"Hey, if you don't want me drawing conclusions, start answering the questions."

She sat back with a huff but set her mind to thinking. Finally, she just sighed and shrugged. "What it all boils down to is...I want a man who's honest, bighearted and hardworking. Who loves me and knows how to be faithful and devoted. I want a man who knows how to smile, even if his isn't the handsomest smile I've ever seen."

She stared at her hands, envisioning the man with whom she could spend a lifetime. "I want a man whose face lights up when he sees me, who looks at me when we're talking instead of at his watch or a beautiful woman standing behind me. A sense of humor would be nice." Aware suddenly of Rick's continued silence, she shifted uncomfortably and glanced at him. "That's about it. Everything else is negotiable."

He watched her, a slight smile on his face, his writing hand unmoving.

"Aren't you going to write any of that down?"

He shook his head, his eyes soft on hers. "Haley, please go out with me. I'm honest, hardworking, goodhearted, all that other stuff. I won't look at my watch or another woman while we're talking. I know I make you laugh." His eyes coaxed hers and, reluctantly, she grinned, remembering his garbage adventures and, more importantly, his ability to laugh at himself. She'd never met anyone quite like Rick before. Maybe he was right. Maybe they deserved a chance to explore where this attraction might lead.

Maybe, just maybe—

7

THE DOORBELL RANG.

Frustrated at the interruption, Haley looked away from the sweet sincerity in Rick's eyes and went to answer the door.

"Mom! What are you doing here?"

The older woman pulled Haley into her arms for an exuberant hug.

After a moment, they drew apart to look at each other, always an unsettling experience for Haley. Looking at her mother was like looking at herself in twenty or so years. Same build, similar features, same hair color—or it used to be. Her mother's reddish brown was turning a coppery color with age and she kept those shiny locks short and sleek. She also dressed more smartly than Haley—professional dress, always camera ready.

"Oh, honey, I know I should have called before dropping in like this, but I wanted to surprise you. As a birthday present to myself."

Haley rolled her eyes and laughed. "Your birthday's not till next month, Mom. And you're always dropping by unexpectedly."

The older woman ignored the last observation. "My birthday wish was to drop in and surprise my daughter and it wouldn't have been a surprise if I'd dropped in on the day of my birthday, would it?" Her voice was eminently reasonable.

Haley just shook her head, smiling. She stepped back so her mother could enter.

The older woman's gaze landed on Rick. "Oh, my. I hope I'm not interrupting anything." She turned bright eyes on her daughter, undoubtedly hoping there was something substantial to interrupt.

Gritting her teeth with the effort, Haley managed to keep an even smile on her face. Her mother was nothing if not obvious. "Mom, I'd like you to meet my neighbor, Rick Samuels. Rick, this is my mother, Clara Watson. You might have seen her on TV lately. She's—"

"—hostess of that local morning talk show. The Show Me Show, right? Yeah, I know all about it." Rick's eyes were narrowed, his jaw tight. "Watson-Watson. I can't believe I never put the two of you together before."

Clara smiled broadly. "You watch my show? Oh, how wonderful."

"Oh, I've seen it. So has most of the city, from what I understand."

Surprised by the sarcastic edge to his voice, Haley glanced at Rick. He seemed actually hostile.

Oblivious, the older woman clapped her hands together. "Oh, I just knew it would be a success. Everything's just going so well. My career is taking off, my daughter is obviously seeing men again." She smiled broadly at the two of them.

"Mom!"

"Oh, Haley. Be practical. Now, Rick, I'm so happy to meet you."

"Mrs. Watson—"

"Oh, please, call me Clara. And what is Rick short for? Richard?"

He paused, obviously torn about something. "It's Maverick, actually, but—"

"How dashing. Haley, you're neighbors with a Maverick Samuels. Doesn't that just sound like an exciting name?"

Haley slid a curious glance at her neighbor. "Oh, very. But, Mom—"

Clara's eyes widened and she held up a hand for silence. "Maverick Samuels. *Maverick Samuels.* Oh, Haley, I'm so proud. I just knew you wouldn't let me down, but I had no idea you'd be this ambitious when you started seeing men again."

"I haven't exactly been in a convent, Mother."

"Close enough, darling." She glanced sideways at her daughter.

Haley propped her hands on her hips. "I date. I *do*. Remember Peter?"

"So where is he?"

Haley dropped her hands. "Not here."

"So we have Rick. Maverick Samuels." Clara rolled the name off her tongue as though finding it absolutely delicious. "Lucky Number Four, right?" She smiled flirtatiously.

Rick glared. "So I heard. Thanks for ruining my life."

Haley frowned and glanced at her mother. "What am I missing here?"

"He was part of that show I put together for you."

Haley's confusion intensified. "What?"

Rick turned the glare on Haley. "I might have known."

"Known what?" Haley's voice was exasperated now.

He sighed in disgust. "Never mind. I'm out of here."

The door slammed behind him and Haley turned questioning eyes on her mother.

Clara shrugged. "All's fair in love and war."

"That's lame. What's going on?"

The older woman sighed. "You know how I always ask when you're going to get married and you always say when you find the right man? Well, I decided to help you out. Subtly. I knew you'd watch my show, or at least I *thought* you would." She eyed her daughter reproachfully.

Haley rolled her eyes. "So I missed a show or two. I'm sorry. I do work, Mom. I catch it when I can, but I can't just leave Jen stranded if we're busy."

"So you say. Well, you missed an important show. My guest was one of the local gossip columnists, and she was kind enough to list ten available, extremely eligible bachelors. Do you remember Adam Harding?" Clara gracefully smoothed invisible creases from her skirt.

"The 'friend' you brought to the store to meet me last time?"

"That's him. He was on the list. Number nine, I think." She glanced back up at her daughter, a bright smile on her face. "Your Rick was number four."

Haley's eyes widened. "Rick's considered 'extremely eligible'? Well, that figures. That's where all the unwelcome women are coming from."

"Only I forget why." She tapped a fingernail to her chin. "It will come to me. He's either rich or well-connected or just plain gorgeous. Well, the answer's right there, I guess." Clara smiled meaningfully at her daughter.

"A hunk. Yes, I know. I have eyes." She scowled, plopping down on the couch. "But I'm not a desperate woman, you know. I can find a man of my own. I don't need my mother to broadcast a list of eligible men for me to try out, for heaven's sake. Besides, your tastes and mine differ drastically these days."

"Not from what I can see." Clara's smile was more womanly than a daughter should have to witness.

"*Eeew.* Yuck. Don't talk like that."

"Oh, Haley. You're too old to be naive. Your generation didn't invent sex, you know."

"We only wish we had," Haley muttered.

"I heard that, young lady. Lucky for you, I'm willing to drop it." Clara seated herself on the couch next to her daughter, carefully crossing one leg over the other. "Because I'm still waiting to hear about Rick."

Haley sighed. "There's nothing to hear, Mom. He's my neighbor and sometimes my friend. Although he probably hates me now that he knows it was my mother who crucified him on TV. For my sake."

"I did not 'crucify' him. It was a favorable mention. I'm surprised his social life hasn't picked up considerably since the show aired."

"Oh, it has. You should see all the women who chase

him. Tall, big-chested and beautiful. If they don't turn him on, you can bet I don't stand a chance."

"Nonsense. Your father was the same way. He was such a ladies' man, all these pretty young things with fluff for brains chasing after him. Oh, I'm sure he enjoyed himself. But once he met me, he turned blind to all the other women. He was faithful to me all the years of our marriage." Clara's eyes were soft with memories.

Haley smiled. Privately, she didn't believe her mother's rose-colored glasses had ever allowed her to see her father's short, rather unremarkable appearance. Clara only remembered the sweet, loving light that had shone from his eyes whenever he looked at her. Haley wanted a man just like him.

"Besides, Haley, an experienced man isn't necessarily a bad thing." Clara nodded wisely at her daughter. "It makes things a lot more interesting in the bedroom if your man's not a complete novice."

Haley clapped her hands over her ears and squeezed her eyes shut. "Mother! I don't want to hear this! Tell me the story about the stork. I liked the stork. I could deal with the stork. It was a nice, sweet story you could tell a child without traumatizing her for life with pictures of her parents in the bedroom—oh, yuck!"

Peeking out of one eye at her mother, Haley saw the wise smile on the older woman's face. Groaning, she stalked upstairs to her bedroom. *Anything* to change the direction of this conversation. A few minutes later, she came back down dressed in jeans and a sweatshirt. She sat on the couch and began tugging on her tennis shoes.

Clara watched her quietly, an amused smile on her face. "I'll play nice now, Haley. Just tell me the truth. Are you seeing Rick? Or some other nice man?"

Haley stood up, a determined smile on her face as she ignored the questions. "Are you up for the usual?"

"Oh, my, yes. Frozen custard sounds wonderful. Now, tell me more about—"

"Good," Haley cut her off, a smile still firmly in place. "It's been ages since I had frozen custard from Ted Drewes. I'm in the mood to splurge."

Thirty minutes later, they were seated on the hood of Haley's little car. Clara, oddly comfortable in her prim little outfit, was busily shoveling a strawberry short-cake concoction between genteelly painted lips.

Haley was enjoying a large mint and chocolate confection with pistachio nuts and a year's worth of calories. After a few minutes, she set it down next to her, moaning with strained satisfaction.

"Haley?" Clara's voice was more tentative than Haley had heard in recent memory. "There's something I need to tell you."

Haley frowned at the unusually hesitant note in her mother's voice. "What is it, Mom?"

"I...well, I'm... Lately, I've been— Oh, I'm *dating*, all right?" She rushed the words out, with equal parts excitement and uncertainty. "I was upset when you first suggested I see men, but the more I thought about it, the more I decided you were right."

Haley just stared.

"I've been putting too much of the burden of my happiness onto your shoulders. No daughter should have to get married and churn out babies just to keep her mother company. That's not right, and I had no business forcing that on you."

Haley's eyes widened further.

"Now, stop that. I make mistakes, too. And I do apologize for them."

Haley nodded, swallowing loudly. "You're dating."

"Yes."

"A man."

"Yes. I'm not a lesbian."

Haley closed her eyes at the visions that ensued. "Oh, yuck."

"So naive." Sighing, Clara shook her head.

Haley took a deep breath, let it out slowly. Tried for a normal, conversational tone. "So, do I know this man?"

Clara glanced away. "Yes, a bit. Not well."

Haley nodded. "Will I get to meet him? At least know his name?"

"I don't know." Clara began twisting her rings on her fingers. First the sapphire, then the diamond, around and around.

"I would like to meet him."

Sapphire, diamond. "Maybe later." Sapphire. "If anything comes of it." Diamond. "I'm just having fun right now." Her fingers stopped, clenched together, and Clara turned a serious gaze back on her daughter. The sadness in her eyes was still very deep. "I loved your father with my whole heart. I don't know that I could ever stop loving him. And I don't know if there's room in my life for another man."

Haley nodded, setting her own discomfort aside. She

hugged her mother. "Take your time. I don't want you to be lonely."

Clara smiled, squeezed her daughter's hands. "And I'll try not to be so pushy with you any anymore, dear. I mean it this time. I won't keep springing available men on you and I'll try not to interfere in your social life. I just can't help but worry about you. It upsets me to think of you alone so much."

Haley saw the genuine concern on her mother's face and sighed. "I'm looking, all right?" She mumbled the words awkwardly.

"What?" Clara sat forward, long nails clicking anxiously against metal. She gazed at her daughter with wide, disbelieving eyes.

Haley picked up her spoon and began licking at the smears of ice cream she'd missed. "I said I was trying to find someone." The words came out muffled.

Clara snatched the spoon out of her daughter's hand with enough energy to make Haley rear back in alarm. "Repeat that. It sounded like..."

Eyeing her mother cautiously, Haley spoke with quiet sincerity. "I said I was trying to find a man. I'm dating, and I guess you could say I'm actively looking. Is that hopeful enough for you?"

"Oh, darling!" Clara wrapped her arms around her daughter and squeezed the breath out of her. "I could be a grandmother by springtime."

"Whoa. Hold on, Mom. I'm not planning on conceiving any babies this week. Or next week. Or even in the next year. I need a man first, remember? One step at a time."

"Oh, but it won't take you any time at all." Clara slid

off the car and turned to her daughter, speaking with quick excitement. "You're a smart, beautiful girl. Any man would be a fool to turn you down."

"Uh, Mom? Remember Peter?"

Clara frowned distractedly. "Peter? What has he to do with anything?"

"Well, we were seeing each other pretty seriously—"

Clara's eyes widened. "Is he the one?"

"Well, I thought he might be, but—"

"Oh, honey! Are you going to marry him?" She gasped.

"No!" Haley's own voice rose in panic.

"Oh." Clara looked at her blankly for a moment, patted at her hair. "Well, I suppose there's always Rick. But if you already had a man willing, why didn't you—"

"Mom, please. That's what I'm trying to tell you. I didn't really have him. I caught the jerk with another woman." She slid off the hood of her car and tossed her cup in the trashcan before facing her mother. "So, you see, your daughter isn't exactly irresistible." Haley's grin felt crooked.

Her mother frowned. "Oh, Haley. I'm sorry, honey."

"It's okay. Really. I'm okay. I guess my point is, it would be easier for me if you wouldn't jump on this project with so much enthusiasm. I'm a little gun-shy still."

Clara brushed at the back of her skirt as she rounded the car to the passenger's side. "Project? That's an odd way of putting it."

Haley rolled her eyes as she opened her car door. "You're not kidding about that, Mother."

SO NOW HE WAS BACK TO BEING a hunk of meat, Rick mused cynically. He sank back in his couch, trying not to remember what had almost happened tonight on another couch.

And before that, what *Selina* had wanted to do to him on *his* couch. It was enough to make a man want to get his furniture steam cleaned.

Selina had been as obvious as all the others. Just a few months ago, the woman had been lukewarm to cold on the few dates they'd shared. Now that Haley's famous mom had aired her infamous show, lukewarm had gone all steamy and aggressive on him.

Rick tossed a chip in his mouth and reached for the remote. A man's true best friend.

As far as he could figure it, the only difference between Selina and Haley, was that Haley's mother was the one with the strong arm. Well, he supposed there might be an IQ differential, and there was the fact that Haley starred in nearly all of his fantasies these days. Selina just didn't bear thinking about.

Still, he couldn't get over the fact that Haley's mom had aimed an entire show at getting her daughter married off to a guy with decent prospects. Now he knew where Haley came by the tendency toward wrong-headed persistence. Lucky for him, mother and daughter hadn't joined forces or he might have found himself well and truly outmaneuvered.

He wondered if Haley's attitude toward him would change now that she knew he was Lucky Number

Four, whose "luck" had translated into a profitable computer chain and a bulging bank account. He'd accomplished all of this at a relatively young age, too, judging by the stats of his peers.

So the big question now was, assuming Haley knew he was rich, would she abandon her geek hunt? Would she start crawling all over him, just like the women who started chasing him after Clara Watson aired that stupid bachelor list on her show?

It was lowering to realize that part of him hoped for exactly that. Part of him would take Haley any way she'd chase him. He frowned. But then, the other part...the other part would be pissed as hell. Talk about confirmation of his worst fears about her. It would be even worse than if she'd just found out about his dorky past and chased him for that reason. At least that demonstrated standards and nonmalicious intent. The other was mercenary. Nah, Haley would be more likely to go for the geek than the rich guy, while Clara would pick the rich guy for her, hands down.

He grimaced, completely disgusted. Really, what it all came down to, was that Haley and Clara Watson, regardless of their motives and intentions, were just two more women out to judge men by what they looked like and what they did for a living. He was sick of it. They both needed a lesson as far as he was concerned.

Rick smiled with grim resolve. And that was exactly what he had in mind for Haley. Greg would arrive tomorrow afternoon...let the lesson begin.

THE NEXT AFTERNOON, Rick left work early, feeling a mix of anticipation and dread. Greg was undoubtedly camped out on his doorstep right now, an opportunity dressed in highwater pants and Coke-bottle glasses. All he had to do was follow through on his bargain with Haley and set her up with a guy he knew, just as she'd asked.

This was his chance to teach Haley a lesson. Gregory, more than anyone he knew, looked like what she might consider a geek. But Rick also knew that almost everything Haley expected to find in her "sweet geek" was missing in his irresponsible but good-hearted cousin.

So he'd set them up together. He grinned. It should prove to be an enlightening experience for her.

But what if she fell for Greg despite his faults?

The grin disappeared. Could he really do that to her? Just to teach her a lesson? And could he put himself through that kind of torture? Watch her date another man?

She wouldn't fall for Greg. Would she? No, of course she wouldn't. Haley was a smart girl. As soon as she dated Greg a couple of times, she'd figure it all out for herself. And maybe then she'd see him—Rick— through unbiased eyes and give him a fair chance. It could work.

As it turned out, Rick didn't need to lift a finger to introduce the prospective couple. He came home to find a hasty note taped to his door advising him to swing by the apartment next door when he got home. Apparently, Greg was getting to know Rick's attractive neighbor.

When Haley opened the door to his knock, Rick

found his cousin happily eating a sandwich on Haley's couch, while poor Sherlock whined away upstairs in the bedroom.

Greg looked up, his eyes sparkling in pleasure behind the thick lenses of his glasses. "Rick. It's good to see you again." He stood up, brushed breadcrumbs off his badly wrinkled pants leg and offered his cousin a hand.

Still taking in the ramifications of the scene before him, Rick shook hands with his cousin and forced a smile. "Greg. Heard you'd be in town today. How have you been?"

Greg shuffled his feet a bit, gestured vaguely with hands that looked too broad for his long, thin arms, then tried a grin. "My sister's kids make enough noise to drown out a jet engine. Let's just say I'm appreciating the quiet. And the company." He smiled at Haley, who returned it easily.

"Great." Rick's smile encompassed the two of them, even as he ignored the uncomfortable twitching in the pit of his stomach. "I see you two have already met. That's great. Greg here is pretty new to the area, Haley." He smiled meaningfully at her.

Up to this point, she'd been watching Rick a bit uneasily. He assumed she was wondering about his reaction to meeting her mother yesterday. When he treated her with nothing but friendly good grace, the wariness disappeared from her expression, replaced by relief, and then overtaken by uneasy comprehension. He was fulfilling his end of their bargain—finding her a man.

Haley's smile tightened, her chin tilted and she

turned back to Greg. "So you're new to St. Louis? It's a great city. I'd be happy to show you around."

"Hey, that would be great. Rick's not much for the nightlife. At least he hasn't been in the past. So what do you say we do something tonight?" Greg's smile was eager.

Haley's brows rose and she replied, a bit distantly. "Tonight? Um, sure. We could do that." She began discussing possibilities with Greg.

Rick leaned against the side of the couch, satisfied. They were well on their way, and if Haley's expression was anything to go by, Greg wasn't quite what she'd expected. In fact, he'd be surprised if his cousin's over-eagerness, not to mention the last-minute invitation, didn't turn her off completely.

He'd also noticed, with mixed feelings, that Haley wasn't jumping to take up her mother's cause. She wasn't pursuing him more now than she had been a week ago. He could only assume that meant her mother's revelation wasn't having the predicted effect on Haley. How…satisfying? Not quite.

It did, however, make him wonder just how much Clara Watson had told her daughter about Lucky Number Four.

Rick cleared his throat. "So, Haley. I guess your mom explained about that stupid bachelor list she aired."

Haley gave him a cautious look. "Somewhat."

"Did she happen to explain how they picked the list of ten out of the entire population of St. Louis?"

Haley rolled her eyes. "A scientific study, I'm sure." Greg snorted and she spared him a slight grin before turning back to Rick. "No, all she told me was that each of the guys was remarkable, either in fortune or looks." She paused. "Looks. Of all things to try to rank." She gazed at Rick in mild speculation. "I mean, there's no denying that you're attractive. But it boggles the mind to wonder how someone would decide who's hot enough to be one of a city's top ten most eligible." She shrugged. "All I can figure is you must have really caught some woman's eye."

"So you think they picked me for looks alone?" Rick gave her an intent look.

She seemed to choose her words carefully. "Well, considering at least one of the other guys was a millionaire... No offense, Rick, but I'd have to say yes. It's hard to compete with a millionaire, no matter how well your bike business is doing."

That said, she turned back to talk more with Greg, leaving Rick to ponder in silence. She didn't know. He'd bet she didn't have a clue that he owned a chain of computer stores. So...nothing lost, nothing gained, he supposed.

Haley's surprised laugh drew his immediate attention. Rick frowned. Surely, the two hadn't been standing so close together a minute ago. Did Greg really need to touch her arm like that?

Not that he blamed his cousin. Haley was downright beautiful when she laughed. He'd dated women who had literally invented their version of a sexy chuckle. Others self-consciously hid laughter behind a raised hand. Not Haley. She laughed joyously, an honest, contagious sound that drew the eye and a responding smile.

Restraining the urge to pummel his cousin and drag Haley off to bed, Rick cleared his throat. "Well, if you're ready, Greg, why don't we get you settled in at my place?"

Still chuckling, Greg nodded distractedly. "Oh, sure. Sure." He continued talking for a few more minutes and Haley gave him her undivided attention.

Rick pointedly opened the door and started out into the hallway, assuming his cousin would eventually follow. Greg did. Slowly. It took another five minutes for him to actually cross the threshold out into the hallway. Once there, he turned to continue chatting with Haley, drawing out the good-byes and call-you-laters.

Gritting his teeth in annoyance, Rick finally gave Greg a not-so-subtle shove to get him moving into the apartment next door. He kicked the door closed behind him and dropped Greg's duffel bag at his feet.

"That Haley's something else, man. Thanks for giving me the opening."

Rick sighed, seeing all his plans going up in flames. "Look, maybe this was a mistake. Maybe you should call Haley and tell her you can't make it tonight."

Greg dropped onto Rick's leather couch and stacked his feet on the coffee table. "Why would I do something stupid like that? Haley seems like a lot of fun."

Rick's frustration boiled over. "Sure she does. And you want to know why she's going out with you? She thinks you're a geek."

Greg stared a moment. "A geek."

"Yeah. A dweeb. Dork. Social misfit. A gullible frog in a world of asshole Prince Charmings." Rick waved off his own words with a disgusted gesture. "Whatever you want to call it. But she's on the hunt for one. Fall into her trap and she'll make you a geek *husband* next."

Dropping his feet off the coffee table, Greg sat forward, the carefree smile fading. "I don't get it."

Briefly, Rick explained Haley's plans. As he wound down and his frustration cooled, Rick felt guilty for exposing her and inadvertently hurting Greg. He still believed what she was doing was wrong, and yet, knowing her, knowing her past and her total lack of malice, he couldn't condemn her as easily as he might have just a few weeks ago. "Look, she's a nice girl. A lot of fun, really, but her ideas are all backward, and I think she needs to figure that out." He shrugged. "But you're my cousin, and I couldn't just offer her your head on a platter."

Greg fidgeted for a moment, yanked off his glasses and swiped them with his shirt, then put them on. He eyed his cousin steadily, his eyes shrewd. "So, maybe that's even more reason why I should go out with her. You and I both know I'm not husband material for any girl." His words were matter-of-fact, his confidence unaffected.

"You don't have to do that, Greg. To be honest, I thought about setting you two up, but—" He sighed. "I guess that's exactly what I did, though, isn't it?"

Greg still watched him, a curious smile spreading across his face. "But you hate the idea of me going out with her. You want her for yourself."

Rick swung away from his cousin, wanting desperately to hit something. "No. She's a nut. She's stubborn, wrongheaded, reckless, a reverse snob. And she's got a pushy mother who's made my life hell the past few weeks. What could I possibly see in her?"

"Oh, boy. You've got it bad."

Rick paused then turned back to face Greg. He gestured aimlessly with one hand, before giving up and nodding. "Yeah." He dropped onto the couch.

"Rotten luck."

Rick grinned and shook his head. "You said it."

"Well, if you like her so much, why don't you just convince her that you're the kind of guy she's looking for? You're more of a computer whiz than I am." He swept a baleful gaze over Rick's physique. "And you weren't always so damn buff. Wear baggy clothes or something and take out the contacts, put your glasses on. All that, together with your lack of anything approaching a social life, might even get you a date with her."

"I can't do it. It just goes against the grain to give in to her brand of snobbery. She doesn't know anything about what I've been or what I've done with my life. And it's going to stay that way unless she decides she wants me no matter what I look like or how I make my living."

Greg frowned, his eyes doubtful. "You sure about that? It doesn't sound like a great way to pick up a girl."

"No, but it's something I have to do." Rick gazed morosely at his feet, propped on the coffee table. He shrugged. "I guess I need to prove to both of us that she's not as shallow as all that."

Greg spoke thoughtfully. "Maybe I can help you out.

Hey, you're putting me up for who knows how long—"

Rick looked up, alarmed at the phrasing. "How long?"

"—and getting me a job—"

"Which you damn well better work at this time—"

"—so how about I go out with Haley and show her a rotten time?"

Rick stared at his cousin. "You're kidding."

Greg shook his head, grinning triumphantly. "Nope. I owe you big. So, how about I go out with your girl for you?"

8

FOR THE REST OF THE AFTERNOON, Rick had second, third, even fourth thoughts about turning Greg loose on poor, unsuspecting Haley. Greg's plan was unassailable. Brilliant even. A subtle, yet clever, twist on Rick's original plan. But was it cruel?

"So how do I look?" Greg held his arms wide and spun around in a gangly imitation of a runway model.

Rick shook his head, grinning in reluctant appreciation. "Terrible. Horrible. Perfect."

Greg was an exaggeration of himself, a compilation of the worst items in his wardrobe, which, when worn separately, looked just a bit off. Worn together, the resulting outfit looked downright odd. Haley would need a strong constitution to go out in public with a man dressed as badly as this.

"Do you know how you're going to act? What you're going to say?" Rick asked. He felt as though he were standing on the edge of a cliff and asking for a push.

"Sure." Greg shrugged casually, his grin reasonably shameless. "Mostly just like myself. Cranked up a notch for good measure."

Rick's amusement faded. "You're not getting a complex on me, are you?"

"Nah. You and I both know we have different philosophies on life. I like to enjoy it and you like to work

it to death." He held up a hand to halt any reproaches.
"But I can work when I need to. And I'll work my tail
off at your computer store. I promise." He grinned.
"I'll work my tail off trying to make a rotten impression on Haley, too. Deal?"

Rick clapped a hand on Greg's thin shoulder and
smiled. "Tell you what. You pull this off, and I'll owe
you one. How's that?"

"Sounds good."

"Okay. Go pick your date up."

"No way. Gotta make that first impression stick. I'm
going to be a good twenty minutes late."

Rick thought of Haley sitting there, watching the
clock, and winced. All in the name of a good cause, he
reassured himself.

NEXT DOOR, HALEY GLANCED at the clock for the fourth
time in the past ten minutes, and started tapping her
toe. Maybe she was old-fashioned, but she thought the
woman should retain the privilege of being late for a
date, not the guy. So far, Greg wasn't making a wonderful impression.

A pathetic whine caught her attention just then, and
Haley turned to look up the stairs at Sherlock, whom
she'd penned into her bedroom again. This time, she'd
taken care to secure valuables and cover all beloved
furniture with old sheets.

Another ten minutes went by before she heard a
knock at the door. With a last warning glance at Sherlock, Haley went to answer it.

What followed was a caricature of a bad date. Greg
insisted on driving her car, parked it illegally in front

of the restaurant, then let the restaurant door slam in her face. When she opened it and stared, waiting for some kind of apology, he just shrugged and looked around the lobby. Spotting a curvy woman with a micromini skirt, he grinned and openly stared at her. Haley watched, sure that he had a punch line or some bit of foolishness to turn the moment into a joke. Nope. The guy was definitely ogling.

During the meal, Greg kept referring to the aphrodisiac quality of some dishes, urged strong drinks on her with an oily grin, and spoke incessantly about other women he'd dated. He considered himself a Don Juan, she noted with surprise.

Unable to listen to any more without making a rude comment, Haley smiled and determinedly changed the subject. "So how long are you in town visiting Rick?"

"Oh, didn't he tell you? I'm moving in. Sort of a longish temporary situation. Until I can get a job and some cash socked away. Then I'll try to find a place of my own." He grinned meaningfully. "I like my privacy."

"Right." She didn't return the smile. "So did you and Rick see a lot of each other growing up?"

Greg shrugged. "More or less. We didn't really have much in common. He's kind of boring. All work and no play. That kind of thing. I believe in enjoying life for what it is. Short and temporary. Kind of like my careers." He grinned and lifted an arm with the obvious intent of hooking an elbow over the back of his chair.

He miscalculated.

That bony elbow slammed into the ribs of an oncoming waitress, whose tray tipped enough to spill half a dozen mugs of coffee onto the floor. In her desperate effort to right the tray before the rest of its contents met the same fate, the waitress juggled and bobbed and finally lost the battle, tripping and sending the tray flying into the next table. Shocked into immobility, Haley watched helplessly as Greg's elbow took out a good fourth of the restaurant.

The horrible crash and clatter ended in a shocked silence that spread throughout the crowded room. Haley froze right along with the rest of the diners, while Greg jumped out of his chair, apologies spewing forth as he crouched to help the waitress up.

"Oh, man. I'm sorry. Here." His cheeks flushed a bright red, Greg gently nudged the flustered and stained waitress into his chair. He used his napkin and an ugly handkerchief from his breast pocket to swab up the mess as best as he could.

Her embarrassment and horror receding, Haley considered Greg from a fresh perspective. True, he'd caused the mess, but it had been an accident and he'd responded with rare gallantry. Sliding back her chair, Haley grabbed her napkin and knelt next to Greg, carefully picking up broken shards and depositing them on the tray Greg had retrieved. Together, they managed to clean up the worst of it before two busboys arrived with mops and dishrags.

His cheeks still flushed and a sheen of sweat glistening on his forehead, Greg grimaced at Haley. "I'm really sorry about all this. If you want to leave now, I'll understand."

She smiled at him, the most genuine expression she'd managed all evening. "Actually, no. Unless you're uncomfortable, I thought maybe we could just finish our dinner." She laughed. "As long as you keep closer tabs on your elbows, that is."

Greg laughed and dropped back into his chair. As the evening wore on, he tossed out a few more obnoxious remarks, but they seemed halfhearted to her. Haley began to wonder if Greg's obnoxious behavior was his way of overcoming shyness or discomfort around women.

Later, after he'd walked her to her door and she turned to face him, she immediately raised her hands in defense. "Hold it, Romeo. I like you, believe it or not." She watched him warily, ready to intercept a clumsy pass.

"But?" He raised innocent eyebrows.

"But that's as far as it's going. Maybe now that we have that out of the way you can drop the act."

"What act?" He blinked behind his thick lenses.

She just watched him, eyes wide with meaning, until his expression eased into more natural lines and he smiled awkwardly at her.

"So you figured me out. I guess I should have known it wouldn't work. Rick had his doubts, too, but—"

Haley backed farther away from him, her smile fading. "Rick. That's right. He set us up."

"Well, yeah, but—"

"And I suppose, helpful guy that he is, he gave you pointers on how to treat a woman on a date?"

"Well, maybe a few, but—"

"Some teacher." Haley's mood slipped even further. "I don't suppose he wove a lesson of subtlety somewhere in between those pickup lines he gave you, did he?"

"Well, not exactly—"

"Figures. Considering the IQ of the women he attracts, I suppose I should have expected his pickup lines to be less than sophisticated. Look, forget everything he taught you, okay? He's way off base, and I have every intention of telling him so the next time I see him." She smiled grimly. "I might even make a special point of it."

When Greg looked as though he was going to defend his cousin, Haley cut him off. "No, never mind. Why don't you come in and I'll tell you how a man should really treat a woman." She unlocked the door and entered the apartment.

Greg paused a moment outside, uneasy.

"Come on." Haley grabbed Greg's wrist and tugged him inside.

Sherlock, who'd been barking since Haley touched the doorknob, began to whine at the sight of his mistress. From this distance, Haley could see where the dog had already made inroads gnawing away at the gate. The contraption would probably collapse the next time she left the stubborn animal alone. "Quiet, Sherlock." The barks and whines settled to a mere whimper or two as the dog dropped to the floor, resting his nose dejectedly on big puppy paws.

Haley turned with a firm smile to her guest. "Why don't you sit down." She gestured to the couch. "Want a soda? Beer?"

"I'm fine, thanks." He settled himself on the couch,

his expression an odd mingling of caution and curiosity.

She dropped into a chair opposite him and faced him squarely. "You know, I started out not liking you at all tonight, Greg. You were inconsiderate and obnoxious, and the constant innuendo really drove me up the wall. But that's not you at all, is it? That kind of stuff might impress some of your guy friends, but not women. You know what impressed me tonight?"

Greg shook his head wordlessly, his eyes fascinated behind the thick lenses of his glasses.

"The way you jumped right up to clean up your own mess after you knocked the waitress over. I think that's probably the real Greg. I liked him. A lot of girls would. Why don't you let me give you some advice. Drop the act and just be yourself." She smiled encouragingly at him.

He fidgeted a bit before folding his arms across his chest and clearing his throat awkwardly. "You really liked that. The sensitive bit."

"Well, of course. There's nothing manly about rudeness. Every girl wants a man who treats people with kindness and respect. Doesn't that make sense?"

"Yes. Yes, I suppose it does."

"Good. So, why don't we put all that behind us and start over?"

Greg's eyes widened again. He had the expression of a small boy sitting up high on one side of a seesaw, wondering if his playmate was going to leap off her side and send him slamming back down to earth. "You want to start over."

"Sure. So tell me about the real Greg. I understand you're a wonder with computers." She grinned at him.

Greg laughed. "Not a wonder, but I know my way around them."

"A bit more than that, I'd bet. So are you a trouble-shooter or do you create software? What do you do?"

And with that they settled into comfortable conversation. As she expected, Haley found Greg to be friendly, pleasant, even shy on occasion. Two hours later, she was stifling a yawn, not out of boredom, but because she'd gotten little sleep last night. Wondering about Rick's reaction to the scene with her mother yesterday had kept her awake and worrying more than she liked.

Seeing her yawn despite her efforts to resist, Greg laughed. "Past your bedtime, I guess?"

Haley grinned. "Sorry. It's not the company, I promise. I enjoyed it, mostly this part of the evening. You're a nice guy, Greg. And before you revert to your Romeo ways, no, that's not an invitation to take me to bed, you stud, you."

Greg laughed and stood up. "Thanks for going out with me, Haley." He shifted awkwardly. "And I'm sorry about earlier. That must have been a drag for you."

"I've had worse dates." She grinned evilly. "Though not many." She walked him to the door, raised on tiptoe to drop a friendly kiss on his cheek, then stepped back so he could open the door.

His cheeks flushed, Greg smiled at her and paused before closing the door behind him. "Haley?"

"Hmm?" She smiled at him, sleep tugging hard at her.

"I know this wasn't exactly the date of your dreams, but...any chance I could take you out again? Make it up to you?"

She paused, her drowsiness fading. "Well..."

"I promise not to act like a jerk next time."

Translation—he would use his own lines, not his cousin's. Well, at least with Greg, she knew what she was getting. Raising her chin, she forced a wide smile. "Sure. I'd love to."

"Great." With another grin and a half-wave, he promised to call and closed the door after himself.

He really was a nice guy, she thought. Easy to talk to, sweet when he forgot himself. He'd make a wonderful brother, a really great husband—for someone else. She sighed.

All she could think about was a pair of blue eyes laughing down at her, seeming to promise all kinds of sinful delights. Just remembering Rick's body pressed against hers, his sensual mouth devouring her own, sent her heart pounding into overdrive. Fickle, fickle heart.

She groaned. How dare he give such horrible instructions to his shy, awkward cousin, anyway. She'd have a thing or two to tell him the next time she saw him. Feeling an ache deep inside, she knew it was more than just anger on his cousin's behalf that drove her.

No, her rebellious heart was breaking. She couldn't bear the idea of Rick giving his cousin instructions on how to seduce her. She'd thought after Rick's description of his ideal woman, and his heartfelt plea to give him a chance, that he might really care about her. Obviously, she was wrong.

Any man who gave another man instructions on how to get the girl couldn't possibly want her for himself.

NEXT DOOR, RICK PACED the floor, waiting and wondering if his plan was working. Surely by now Haley had seen the error in her thinking. Greg might look the part of her responsible, good-hearted geek, but he was as flighty as a bored debutante. When the door opened and Greg strode in, whistling, Rick whirled to face him.

Greg looked up, halting in mid-whistle. "Um, Rick. Hi. You're still up."

"And waiting for you. So what happened? Did she slug you? Throw you out?"

Greg averted his eyes. "Not exactly."

Rick paused in sudden suspicion.

At Rick's hard stare, Greg backed up a pace. "Look, I'm sorry. I know I promised to turn it up a notch and act like the biggest macho jerk she ever laid eyes on, and I really tried but I didn't have the heart for it. She's a nice girl." He raised his chin and eyed Rick squarely. "I liked her. I wouldn't mind dating her myself."

"You *what*?"

"I said I liked her."

Rick kept his approach calm and steady. He silently swore not to cause any lasting injury. "I see. And Haley wasn't turned off by the macho jerk act."

"Well, she was, but," Greg infused some charm into his smile, "she kind of saw through my act. She thinks I'm a nice guy who puts on an act out of shyness."

Rick nodded knowingly, his temper seething. "Yes, I've seen you try the shy, misunderstood act on other girls. It's very convincing."

Greg gave a halfhearted laugh. "Um, well, sure. But this time it wasn't all an act. She really caught me out."

Rick nodded, his smile hard. "She thinks you're shy. And you say it wasn't an act. Pull the other one, cuz."

The smaller man grinned sheepishly. "Okay, so maybe I played that up. She looked so sympathetic that it was too hard to resist. But it wasn't that far from the truth. I know you think I'm a screw-up, but I think I could turn myself into an upright kind of guy for the right girl."

Rick nodded expressionlessly. "And you think Haley could be the right girl."

Greg shrugged, his grin in place, though his eyes flickered nervously. "She could be."

"She's not, Greg. You snowed her. It's not the way we agreed you'd snow her, but you still put on an act for her. That's not how you attract a girl you want to build something serious with."

Greg stood his ground against his much larger cousin. "Why not? That's what you did."

Rick stopped. "It's not the same thing." So why did it feel so wrong suddenly?

"Sure it is. You pretended to be something you're not because you're afraid she's going to take advantage of you. Then you have me put on an act so she'll turn to you. Looks to me like you snowed her worse than I did."

Greg raised his chin. "And you know what else? You keep harping on Haley being the one full of stereotypes and pegging people, but has it occurred to you that that's exactly what you did to her? You stereotyped her. You grouped her in with all these women who started chasing you once you struck it rich. Now, maybe she might have acted that way, given the chance, but you never did give her that chance. You just *assumed*. Now, man, if that ain't stereotyping, then I don't know what is."

As much as he'd like to strangle his cousin, Rick had to admit, at least to himself, that Greg had a point. Maybe even a couple of them. He stared a moment longer, then turned without a word to go back to his bedroom.

YEP, THIS WAS ABOUT AS LOW as a guy could go, Rick decided. Here he was, spying on his neighbor and his own cousin, on a date he'd all but engineered. Hell, he couldn't believe they were still dating. Why was she doing it, anyway? To spite him? Because she was desperate? Now all he could think about was how to break the pair up.

He took another swig of beer then set the bottle down on the bar. He kept a covert watch on the couple chatting on the other side of the room.

"Hi." The voice was low and smoky, belonging to someone he'd only vaguely noticed sitting down next to him.

He glanced over, noted the classic good looks of the woman seated next to him. "Hi." A year ago, he might have taken the woman up on the invitation in her eyes.

"Could I buy you a drink?"

"I'm all right, thanks." He smiled briefly, then trained his eyes across the room once more.

"She must be quite something."

"Hmm?" He glanced at the woman, who was smiling humorlessly at him.

"The woman you keep staring at."

Uncomfortable, he glanced at his beer and shrugged. "She's with another man."

He maintained his silence, his eyes straying back to Haley, his ears straining to pick up their conversation.

"Want some advice?"

He glanced over at the woman.

She smiled. "If you really care about her, don't keep it a secret from her. Women have a big problem with men who lie to them."

Rick sighed, tried for a smile. "You think so?"

"I know so. Personal experience." Her smile twisted and she took a sip of her drink. "I'm Tawny, by the way."

Rick's eyes widened. *No. Couldn't be.* "Rick. Thanks for the advice, Tawny."

She nodded.

Whoever she was, the woman did have a point. The longer he kept deceiving Haley, the worse his chances would be in the long run. He stood up, his gaze trained on Haley once more. He'd go to her, tell her setting her up with Greg had been a really bad idea, then they'd sit down and have a long talk. About careers, the past, everything.

Just as he turned to go, the woman slid off her own stool, teetering for a moment on high heels. Instinctively, he grabbed her arm to steady her, and she dropped her glass. It shattered on the floor, drawing attention.

Rick looked up, saw Haley and Greg staring at him in shock. Haley's gaze slid to the woman whose arm he still held, and he saw her eyes widen farther. The glare she turned on him was the coldest he'd seen yet. She whispered something to Greg and stood up.

Rick made as if to dodge around Tawny to go to Haley, but the woman held on to his arm for balance as she lifted her foot to inspect her shoe for damage.

When he finally disentangled himself from the woman, it was to see the back of Greg heading out the door. He supposed he could sprint to follow them, but considering Haley lived next door and Greg was his roommate, it seemed a pointless effort. He'd corner them back at home.

"OH, OF ALL THE PEOPLE for him to date. He just had to pick *Tawny*. The nerve!" She'd wanted to hurl something when she saw Rick with his hands all over the woman.

Vaguely, around her own rage, Haley registered the fact that Greg was holding on to his door handle with one hand and had the other braced ahead of him, as though to catch the dashboard at any sudden collision. She let up on the gas pedal.

"What is she, some siren men can't resist? Is it that she's beautiful and available? Well, of course, that would do it. But why is she always picking on the men I—" She caught herself. Rick wasn't her boyfriend, never had been.

She felt eyes on her and glanced at Greg. He looked

pale. She lifted her foot up a bit more, watching as the blur outside of her window separated into buildings, trees, houses. "Sorry."

He cleared his throat. "No harm done. So, um, who's Tawny?"

Haley weighed her words, searching for the most ladylike way of explaining. "Tawny is the woman my ex-boyfriend preferred over me."

"Oh. Sorry." He shifted around in his seat.

"It's not your fault your cousin has bad taste."

"No, I guess not." He paused. "So you didn't like seeing Rick with her."

Haley raised her chin. "I don't like seeing her, period."

He nodded. "That's all it is? She bothers you?"

"Isn't that enough?" She glanced at him, feeling her temper stir again.

"Oh, that's plenty. She's gone."

"For now. But if your cousin starts dating her, I'll probably end up running into her more often." Her stomach tightened painfully at the idea. God, if she had to actually watch Rick with his hands on the woman, she wasn't sure she could keep her claws to herself.

What was she thinking? Rick wasn't hers. She didn't have any claim on him. Angrily, Haley set aside her claws. No, she just didn't want to see the woman, period. Thank God she'd never gotten involved with Rick. No, she had Greg now. They weren't perfect together, but at least he didn't have women chasing him and tempting him with suggestive notes.

"Want to go out with me again?"

Haley smiled grimly. "I'd love to."

A FEW DAYS LATER, limping slightly, Haley wheeled her bike into the bicycle shop, feeling muddy and on the brink of tears.

"Haley! Jeez, what happened to you?" Rick rushed over and took the bike from her. He propped it against a bench then turned a concerned gaze to her scraped and bleeding elbows and knee. She knew her neon green T-shirt and short blue jean skirt were covered in mud, as were her little plaid tennis shoes.

"A combination of a skateboarder and balding tires, I guess." She sighed. "He came out of nowhere and I just couldn't stop. My bike hit a tree." She turned to eye her bike sadly, vaguely aware of Rick motioning away a young man who appeared to work there with him. The co-worker smiled slightly then moved off to help a customer sort through a display of bike helmets.

"Honey, don't worry about the bike. I'll fix it for you. Why don't you sit down and let me take care of the scrapes now."

"No, I'm okay. I have some bandages back at The Toy Boxx. But the bike—" She glanced back at it.

"Haley." He waited for her gaze to swing back to him. "I said I'll fix the bike. Now come with me. No arguments. I'm not sending you away bleeding." He tried a smile. "It goes against store policy."

Weakening, she let him lead her to a chair in the back. He rifled through drawers and cabinets before he found a first aid kit. "Let's see what we got here."

She nodded, feeling self-conscious. Well, maybe not as idiotic as she'd felt facedown on the ground with her bike wrapped around a tree and the wheels still spinning crazily. Only God knows how many people she'd flashed when she fell. That would teach her to go biking in a skirt.

While Haley silently relived her biking accident, Rick began cleaning off her scrapes, dabbing lightly with gauze and antiseptic. When she winced at the sting to her knee, he bent over and blew on it for her, his eyes on hers, gauging her pain. Despite the discomfort, Haley felt shivers working up and down her spine at the warmth of his breath on her bare skin.

As the pain eased, she forced herself to relax.

"Better?" he asked in a husky voice. His fingertips still hovered around her knee and the stretch of bare thigh above it, where her skirt had hiked up when she sat down.

She nodded wordlessly.

Gently, he dabbed ointment on the wound then covered it with a bandage. Then he turned his attention to the smaller scrapes on her elbows, dragging the crate on which he sat just a bit closer to her chair.

He cradled her forearm in one hand and her upper arm in the other so he could inspect the wound. Haley tried not to feel the way her senses focused on those sensitive points of contact. Or the way her breathing was growing shallow, her heartbeat erratic. She cleared her throat, relieved when he applied first one bandage and then the other. He sat back and eyed his handiwork.

"Thank you."

"No problem. That's what friends are for, right?" His grin was lopsided.

She glanced away. "I guess so." She cleared her throat before looking back at him.

He stared into her eyes, his gaze direct. "I saw you the other night with Greg. I was following you."

Her eyes widened. "I see."

"A lady sitting next to me at the bar suggested I not lie to you about it."

Haley raised her chin at the term *lady*. "I'm sure she would know."

He raised an eyebrow. "That's exactly what she said."

Haley shrugged and took the high road. "Your social life is none of my business."

He sat back, a curious smile on his face. "Well, what do you know. It was the same Tawny, wasn't it?"

"I don't know what you're talking about."

"Yes, you do." His smile hardened. "And now, because you saw me with her, you think I'm just like the infamous ex-boyfriend who always did his best work at the office."

Haley felt her temper flare at the reminder of that humiliating incident. She controlled it. "Like I said, it's none of my business. Frankly, I have my own social life to occupy me. Greg and I are dating. I've been meaning to thank you for introducing us. I take it you're happily dating, too, and no longer need my matchmaking services?"

Rick ignored her question. "You wanted to thank me? For introducing you to *Greg*? It looks like I gave you too much credit for common sense."

"Obviously. Well." She stood up. "How much do I owe you for the first aid and the bike?"

His eyes narrowed. "The first aid was on the house.

We'll have to see about the bike. I'll let you know when it's ready."

"Fine."

"Fine."

She smiled tightly, then limped out.

"Yep, I think you've got something there, cuz." Rick grinned at the fantastic display on the computer screen. They were sitting in his office, after hours, because Greg had finally perfected a program he'd been tackling on his own time. Rick was impressed. "I've never seen anything like it."

Greg laughed. "I just hope everyone else thinks so, too."

Rick clapped him on the shoulder. "They will."

Greg grinned then eyed his cousin speculatively.

"What?"

"Um, I understand you still have a manager's position to fill here."

Rick paused, surprised. "Yeah, I do."

"Well, I'm interested, unless you have somebody else in mind."

Rick eyed him curiously. "I asked Tim if he wanted the position, but he won't have the time for the extra responsibility. He's still working on his degree."

Greg took a deep breath. "So, it's still open. What sort of qualifications are you looking for?"

"It's all pretty straightforward really. I need someone who's good with computers, good at dealing with people—and reliable." He left the rest unsaid, just raised an eyebrow.

Greg flushed. "Look, I know I haven't been reliable

in the past, but you had me filing and answering phones back then. I barely got to touch the computers."

Rick shrugged. "I couldn't promote you above my other employees if you couldn't be bothered to show up on time for work."

"Yeah, I know that now." Greg sighed.

"Believe it or not, I'm inclined to agree with you." Rick spoke slowly. "You've been on time every day since you started working at this store. Granted, it's only been a few weeks now, but you have put in your share of overtime and more. That's new from you, as is the positive attitude. You act like a professional. And, I have to admit—" Rick shrugged. "You really are hell on wheels with a computer."

"So?"

"So," Rick paused, smiling, "I have a manager's position to fill. You interested?"

Greg grinned. "Very."

Rick laughed. "All right. The position's yours. Don't fail me."

"I won't. I promise." The words rang with enthusiasm.

"I hope like hell that means you're moving out soon." Rick's words were heartfelt. Greg was a slob.

The younger man laughed, nodding. "As soon as I find my own place."

"Thank God." He chuckled. "I'm kidding. Take your time."

While Greg turned back to the computer, Rick shoved his hands in his pockets, his thoughts turning. "I guess Haley will be glad to hear you're staying on for a while."

"I guess." Greg shrugged, his hands busy at the keyboard.

"You guess?"

"Yeah. To be honest, I think she'll be pleased for me, but I don't think it would devastate her to see me leave either."

"Really."

Greg glanced over his shoulder. "Oh, I didn't mean that the way it sounded. I think she considers me a friend maybe, but that's probably as far as it will ever go." His grin was a bit wistful. "She's a great girl, but I get the feeling she's distracted by something—or some*one*." He exited the program then swiveled his chair to face Rick. "She watches you, man. Not me. You."

Rick froze.

"If you want her, maybe you ought to do something about it."

Rick stared, his thoughts tumbling over each other. The possibilities.

Greg shrugged and grinned.

Slowly, Rick smiled.

9

RICK SHIFTED HIS WEIGHT restlessly, lifted a hand to knock and then dropped it, before lifting it again and rapping sharply. There was no help for it. He needed to come clean with Haley. She deserved the truth. All of it.

And then, to borrow a phrase from his cousin, who seemed to be getting smarter all the time, he was going to do something about his feelings for this woman. He was crazy about her. Her freckles, her boundless enthusiasm for life, even her crazy, backward notions. He only hoped Greg was right. Did she really watch him? Rick pondered that wonderful possibility until the door opened.

"Rick." Haley leaned against the doorjamb, her gaze remote until she spotted the gleaming bike he'd wheeled to her door. "Hey, you fixed it." She smiled.

His lips curved in response to her honest pleasure. "Yeah, it wasn't really so bad. Stan's going to total your bill and mail it to you, if that's okay. Shouldn't be too ugly. I just didn't want you to have to go without wheels again in the morning."

Haley stepped back, let him wheel the bike into the laundry room. "Thanks, I appreciate it."

"Sure, no problem. So how's the knee?"

"Oh, fine. Just a scrape. Thanks for your help the other day."

"I'm just glad you're okay." He shuffled his feet, then caught sight of the leash hanging from the laundry room door. "I thought I could take the dog out for some practice, if it's okay."

"Oh, sure."

When Rick showed the leash to Sherlock, the dog bounded in circles at his feet. A few quiet words from Rick and the dog sat still and waited calmly for Rick to hook the leash to his collar.

Rick eyed the cooperative dog with something less than friendly feelings. *Come on, buddy. You're not helping me out here. You behave too well, and she's not going to need me anymore. Eat any shoes lately?* He paused, sighing in defeat. *When you come clean, you gotta start somewhere.*

"Sherlock's come a long way. He's a smart dog. Has he been giving you any problems?"

"The gate's a mess, but my shoes are faring much better."

He nodded, forced himself to broach the subject. "I guess that means his lessons are starting to sink in. Maybe it's time for you two to go it alone."

Her eyes widened and she shook her head wordlessly. After a moment, she cleared her throat and smiled. The expression seemed forced. "Oh, I don't know about that. He— Well, he ran into the street the other day, and it took several calls before he responded to me. That's kind of dangerous, you know. Dogs get hit by cars all the time."

He studied her thoughtfully, heartened by her obvious reluctance to break this connection between them. Or, maybe she just didn't trust her ability to finish training her dog. "A dog does need to respond immediately to a command like that."

"Exactly. For his own safety."

"His safety," Rick murmured.

"Right." She fidgeted, seeming not to know what to do with her hands. She bent and started petting Sherlock.

"No problem. We'll just continue the training for a while."

She flashed a smile up at him.

Catching himself staring, Rick shuffled then gestured awkwardly between dog and door. "Guess I'd better get started."

Once the door closed behind them, Haley whirled around and leaned against it. She was acting like a hormonal teenager riding high on her first wild crush. Okay, so maybe she'd had a few hot—make that *scorching*—dreams about the guy last night. No reason to act so crazy around him.

She just couldn't seem to get past the feel of his fingers gently tending to her scrapes, brushing against her thigh just below the hem of her skirt. In her fantasies, his fingers had strayed well above her scraped knee, and pretty soon the hem of her skirt had hardly been an issue. And she kept seeing him, minus the tight jeans and T-shirt, with his hands playing all over her body.

She needed to get over it before he realized how susceptible she was right now. She'd end up flat on her back before she remembered what an insensitive clod he really was.

Haley frowned, recalling that moment in the restaurant when she'd looked up and seen him with Tawny at the bar, his hand on her arm. That one relatively innocent moment had been more painful to witness than the sight of Peter literally in the act.

Shying away from the implications of that newfound knowledge, Haley reflected on her conversation with Rick at the bike shop. At the time, she'd been uneasy, then annoyed and hurt. Now she was confused. Rick had never actually verified anything. Still, he'd let her assume he was dating the woman now.

How could he? Now that he knew who Tawny was, friendship alone should put her way out of bounds for him. Shouldn't it? He couldn't be *that* insensitive.

No, he wasn't insensitive. She remembered the gentleness of his touch while he tended to her scrapes. She swallowed heavily as another, even more provocative memory flickered.

Had he really followed her and Greg to the restaurant like he'd said? The very idea was enough to send her heart into a tailspin. No doubt her head and every shred of reason would soon follow.

She squeezed her eyes shut, battling the euphoria back down. How could she possibly trust this silly little voice inside that sang out that Rick was everything she hoped he was? There was so much evidence against him. The note, the women at his door, Serena or Selina or whoever she was, Tawny. Heaven knew his looks alone were enough to render him suspicious in her eyes—or they should be.

Stupid, fickle heart, she grumbled silently, peeling herself off the door. She needed to get busy doing something before Rick came back and found her leaning against the door like a limp noodle.

Twenty minutes later, Rick was back, dog bouncing in behind him. He freed Sherlock then turned to Haley. "So, how are things going with Greg?"

"Fine. Your cousin's a nice guy. How's Tawny?" She all but choked on the woman's name.

Rick eyed her silently for a moment. "I don't know. I only met her briefly at the bar."

Haley swallowed. Hard. Still, she managed to keep her voice even. "Ah, this sounds familiar."

"But true. She was just at the bar. I wasn't dating her. I don't *want* to date her. I was just ticked at you for preferring Greg to me, so I let you believe I was seeing her. I'm not."

Yet another coincidence explained away. She wanted so badly to believe him, but—

"I'm not getting anywhere with you, am I?" He shifted, his stance widening in subtle challenge.

"You don't have to get anywhere with me. We're just neighbors. I'm dating Greg, remember?" Haley was impressed with the even tone of her voice. Maybe Rick wouldn't see how much his words tempted her to abandon reason and rub all over him like a cat.

"Greg. Right. So, is he everything you'd hoped?" Rick's smile was faint, his eyes sharp.

"He seemed a little flustered on our first date, but once he warmed up and started really talking, I could tell he was just a little uncomfortable socially." Remembering the "advice" Rick apparently had given his poor cousin, Haley flashed a brilliantly false smile and verbally dug in her claws. "And boy is that a change from the kind of guy I usually date. Shyness can be so refreshing when you're used to *conceited, arrogant jerks who like to judge everyone but don't hold themselves to the same standards.*"

Rick ignored her hostility, his voice and smile like sunshine. "Well, hey, that's great. So you're going to keep dating him?"

She kept her smile in place. "Sure. Why not? I think he's a viable candidate, don't you?"

His smile changed, his eyes darkening. "'Why not?' How about because you aren't even attracted to him? He just fits into the mold. And that's all you see. The glasses, the computer skills, the weird clothes."

She retreated a pace, her nerves shrieking all kinds of warning messages to her brain. Realizing what she was doing, she held her ground and met his eyes in challenge. "How do you know I don't find him attractive? He's funny, smart, kind. He's *sincere.* Those qualities are much more important that a handsome face or a-an *athletic* body."

"So you like him. You're going to keep seeing him."

Feeling her courage falter, she swallowed and forced a reckless grin. "Right. Like I said, why not?" Since Rick was only a few inches away now, she had to tip her head back to look up at him. She could feel the heat of his body, see the shadow of a beard that would be several shades darker than his hair.

More than that, she felt the pull of his gaze, gone navy blue with the intensity of his emotions. Her breathing quickened. Her body threatened to lean in to his.

She saw his nostrils flare as he read the wanting in her eyes. In a smooth rush, he slid his arms around her and pulled her flush against his body. She could have wept, it felt so good.

He bent toward her, his lips drawing her gaze. She watched them curve subtly before he spoke. "I'll tell you why not. You might *like* him, but you *want* me."

Drugged by the feel of his hard length against her, she only vaguely registered his reply. She felt her body succumbing, melding into him and waiting. She needed— With a groan, she dragged his mouth down to hers.

A masculine sound of approval echoed from deep in his throat and he welcomed her greedy kiss, tongues and lips questing and hungry. Even as she gave herself up to the heat of him, some place deep within her registered the rightness of their fit. Their bodies attracted and came together in a seamless embrace that felt irresistible.

"You feel. So good." She whispered the words brokenly against his mouth. "Oh, I want—"

Her undisguised need seemed to sap any remnants of his anger. "I know, baby." His voice was husky, his hands moving over her slender body, seeking out the aches to soothe and torment.

She moved against him, her fingers roaming his back and lower, to sink greedily into the tight, denim-covered butt she'd been coveting shamelessly for too long now. Their pace grew reckless and she arched against him.

Just as her clothes began to feel too confining, long, hard fingers plucked at their fastenings, exposing naked flesh to a rapt gaze, a tender touch. It slowed her headlong rush to fulfillment. This vulnerability to him was unexpected.

She swallowed heavily, her breathing shallow. "Rick?" It was barely a whisper, hesitant.

"Shh." He touched his lips to hers, brushed his knuckles lightly against her throat.

With that light caress, she recognized the tremors in his hands, which matched the quaking in her stomach and in her soul. His patience despite the hunger they shared spoke of a depth of feeling she hardly dared to name.

Up to this moment, she'd imagined her subtle curves would only disappoint a man as experienced as Rick. But he explored her body tenderly, his hands hot and slow. Savoring. Where she'd expected cool finesse, she found a sweet cherishing that momentarily silenced her doubts.

As though sensing her vulnerability and seeking to offset it, he tugged his shirt over his head and caught her restless hands. He drew them to the button of his jeans.

It was an invitation to adventure. He smiled, his eyes twinkling devilishly.

That teasing challenge eased away the rest of her uncertainty, and she let a grin steal across her lips. She narrowed her eyes at him in warning and he chuckled.

The laugh ended in a whispered curse as she let her fingernails trail teasingly over the teeth of his zipper.

She could only imagine how the mini-vibrations felt against sensitive skin.

Carefully, she unfastened and tugged his jeans and boxers off, then eased back a few inches to gaze upon her new playground. Her eyes widened. "Oh. My." The view was incredible, the possibilities...huge.

He let out a surprised laugh at her undisguised enthusiasm, his cheeks reddening.

She grinned teasingly. "Rick. You're blushing."

His eyes narrowed over the ruddiness of his cheeks. "Shameless hussy."

"And you love it."

"You bet I do." He met her eyes with a direct stare that disarmed. Then he smiled.

Wonderingly, she reached up to touch his face. His gaze darkened and held. He laid a hand over the one she held to his cheek then eased backward, using the connection to draw her with him to the couch. He lowered himself onto it, tugging her to stand between his thighs.

She felt exposed, standing there naked and jittery with nerves and arousal. The gentle swell of her breasts trembled mere inches from glittering blue eyes that regarded her steadily.

With one finger, he traced a coral tip, watching in fascination as it budded beneath his touch. Gently, he repeated the caress, his attention on her response. Her body gradually arched closer, begging for more, for lips, for tongue. Anything. He withheld all but that one fingertip until she couldn't bear it any longer and dragged his head close on a groan of frustration. "Call *me* shameless...would you—ooh..."

Shifting their weight, he laid her on the couch, his lips and tongue merciless. Her world spun and blurred into a dizzy focus that included only this man who seemed to see and feel only her. Helplessly, she felt her heart falter and weaken, stumble and fall.

For her, the search was over. It was this man or nothing. She froze at the knowledge. Her hands, which had been playing restlessly over the sinews of his back, clenched and clung as though to halt time just for a moment so she could adjust.

He pulled back slightly, his breathing ragged, eyes dark and searching. "Haley? Are you okay?" He inhaled roughly, obviously fighting for control. "Do you want to stop?"

Hearing the concern in his voice, and even more, his willingness, despite his obvious need, to stop then and there if it was wrong for her, she steadied. This was Rick. Sexy and charming, yes. Endlessly, arrogantly provoking, also true. But right now, his eyes spoke of a tender sweetness, a depth of soul that was irresistible. Meeting his eyes without flinching, Haley smiled up at him and tugged him back into her arms.

With a groan of thanksgiving, he crushed her body into the cushions, his mouth hungry on hers as he burrowed his fingers into her hair. His hips rocked against her, his throbbing heat scorching the bare skin of her thighs. Her legs moved restlessly beneath his weight, the tension in her belly building into something so sweetly painful she dug her nails into the hard sinews of his flanks.

Reacting as though to fire, he reared up against the urge to plunge deeply, repeatedly. He backed off, his jaw tight and eyes glittering. Feeling the loss, she reached for him, but he shook his head slightly, a wicked twist to his lips. Seeing that sensual curve, she inhaled sharply, anticipating.

Her thigh still trapped beneath one of his, Haley watched with helpless excitement as he drew patterns along the delicate flesh of her thighs. His gaze was demanding. He wanted her to see him, she realized. She would watch him drive her wild and he would see the wildness in her eyes as she grew hotter and more desperate.

Finally, those clever, clever fingers reached the very heart of her desire. The direct contact, amplified by the desire in their locked gazes, sent her shuddering into oblivion.

As he gentled her with caressing hands, easing her back down, she drifted a few moments, her eyes heavy but still staring into his. His gaze, hotter now than before, held such fascination she could feel her belly tightening all over again. She caught her breath at the smile, so filled with intent.

Seeing that arrogance, she fought to reclaim her senses. She smiled slowly. Sitting up, she pushed him backward until he was reclining against the arm of the couch. He moved as if to tug her beneath him, but she held fast.

"Oh, no, you don't." She whispered the words deliberately. "My turn."

His eyes glazed slightly over a widening grin. "By all means—" The last was muffled against her lips as she took his mouth in a deep, carnal kiss that sent the adrenaline rush of power surging through her body.

She laughed into his mouth and let her hands play over the fascinating planes and ridges of his chest and ribs, flat belly and slowly, gradually, lower.

Finally, his eyes blazing and desperate, he grabbed her wrists and clasped them in one hand to prevent any further taunting and dug through the pocket of his discarded jeans. He pulled out a foil packet, presented it to her before releasing her wrists.

Grinning, she managed to extend even that simple act into an exercise in prolonged torture. The moment he was securely sheathed, he flipped her onto her back, surprising a shout of laughter from her. In one swift move, he pinned her arms over her head, and thrust deeply inside her. The suddenness of his entry rocked her with white-hot pleasure, drawing out her laughter into moans of pleasure. She convulsed violently beneath him. Her climax sent him over the top almost immediately until, with one last, deep thrust, he collapsed onto her, burying his face in the moist warmth of her neck.

As her wildly spinning universe eased to a less dizzying whirl, her pounding heart slowed. Gradually, as her tremors eased and her skin cooled, Haley grew aware of a sickening uncertainty in the pit of her stomach. The discomfort built as reality forced its way back into her consciousness.

She'd done it now. So much for her resolve. So much for finding a solid, thoughtful—safe—man to marry. No sweet geek would do now, because here she was, sweaty and naked in the arms of the most gorgeous man she'd ever met.

And she was in love with him.

Haley squeezed her eyes shut, felt her throat tighten. This one was really going to hurt. She just knew it. He was sexy and funny, even heartbreakingly sweet. But hadn't they all seemed that way at first? Before the infatuation wore off and she saw clearly for the first time?

As she knew only too well, charm and good looks could really mask a man's character when a woman was blinded by what she wanted to see. And she so wanted to see good in Rick.

For the first time in her life, she was in love, really, truly in love, and it scared her to death. If infatuation had clouded her judgment before, love would probably obliterate it.

"Ow. Retract, retract." Rick pushed up onto his elbows, dislodging the fingernails that had curled into his shoulders as Haley's tension increased.

"Sorry. I—" Feeling uncomfortably naked beneath his gaze, she glanced away.

He frowned. "What's wrong?"

"I—nothing. Just awkward, I guess." Squelching an unaccustomed need to cling, she pushed lightly against his chest until he rolled to the side. She slid off the couch. Glancing around, she found her T-shirt and slipped it over her head, smoothing it down to her thighs. She fidgeted, wanting to dress, wanting to deny—

"Something's wrong. Did I do something wrong? God, did I hurt you? I know we were kind of wild...." Rick rolled off the couch to stand before her, unconcerned with his nudity.

Her resolve strengthened, though her heart began to

crack, just a little. A man who could be so comfortable in his own skin must have shared himself with a number of women. Who was she to think he could possibly fall for her and her alone? The faces of all the beautiful women she'd seen throwing themselves at Rick paraded through her mind. She didn't stand a chance.

"No, no, of course not. You didn't hurt me. It was..." She forced a smile past paralyzed facial muscles. "It was fun." That was the way to play it. Even if it ripped her heart out, she'd play this casually—just as casually as he probably played it.

Rick stilled. "Fun? So this was fun."

"Oh, loads of fun. But you have to go now." Her smile was starting to crack around the edges.

"Go? Now? After we—"

"I'm afraid so. You know how it is." She bobbed around maniacally, plucking up jeans and shirt and shoes, shoving the bundle at him without glancing down—

He accepted them, eyes wide and alarmed. "Haley, wait. We need to talk."

"Talk? We just did." She tugged Rick toward the door. "Right before the sex part. And even a little after."

"But what about that sex part? I mean—"

Haley wrenched the door open, her smile crumbling by the moment. She couldn't let him see it. And she sure as hell couldn't dig herself in any deeper. He had to go. Now. "It was..." She inhaled sharply, her eyes wide to keep the tears from falling. "A really wonderful...mistake. Goodbye, Rick."

Rick stared, obviously floored. She took the opportunity to nudge him that last step into the hallway, then she slammed and locked the door.

Rick stared speechlessly at the door. "Wonderful? *Mistake?*" He pounded grimly on the door. "Haley. Haley, let me in. That was *not* a mistake. Haley. Answer the door, damn it." He paused. No answer. "You can't just leave me hanging like this. Not after—"

A sudden gasp behind him had Rick whirling around. An older woman he recognized from down the hall stared, goggle-eyed, at his—

He yanked his wadded clothes back to groin level, feeling his cheeks reddening. "Um, sorry. Ma'am."

Her mouth opened and closed like a landed trout's before she found warbly speech. "'Hanging like this,' indeed. If you need to flash your privates at people, go do it downtown. Not around decent folk."

"Yes, ma'am."

Chest burning and belly roiling, he scrambled quickly into his pants, mumbling under his breath. The older woman took her sweet time finding the staircase, seeming only to vanish from sight once Rick's bare ass did.

He raked through his pockets for his keys, ignoring the woman to think about an even more infuriating woman who seemed to consider the best lovemaking of his life to be a "wonderful mistake." What the hell did that mean anyway?

What had gone wrong? Ten minutes ago, he'd believed everything was settled between them. No woman had ever affected him like this. He'd been as rattled as a fifteen-year-old with his first steady girlfriend, trembling with nerves and so damned aroused he'd worried he wouldn't last long enough to satisfy her. For some crazy reason, he'd assumed she felt the same way.

Could he have been so wrong? The tenderness he'd seen in her eyes, the intensity. They amounted to more than sexual attraction, didn't they? Had he been seeing only what he wanted to see? Had he seen love in her eyes just because he'd fallen so completely in love with her?

They'd never said the words.

Maybe she'd just been using him for sex while she looked elsewhere for a serious relationship. Hell, that wouldn't work. If he had anything to say about it, she wouldn't be looking anywhere but in his direction for a serious relationship.

Okay, so they had a few things they needed to talk about. Things like his job and, well, the set-up with Greg. But they'd get past that. He knew they could, if she just gave him a chance.

"So LET ME GET THIS STRAIGHT. You slept with Rick then kicked him out and left him naked in the hallway." Jen watched her, eyebrows raised in disbelief.

Haley winced. "I didn't realize...at the time...that he was naked. I don't know. I was nuts. I didn't do that part on purpose." No, she'd run upstairs and buried her head under a pillow to let the tears fall. Finally. She closed her eyes, her head pounding from the crying and the mental seesawing that had tormented her since Rick left her apartment yesterday. She wanted to believe...but how could she possibly...

She groaned. *Get a clue, Haley.* Just this morning as

she was leaving her apartment—at the crack of dawn so she wouldn't accidentally run into her neighbor—she'd heard a door open. Ducking around the corner, she'd spied yet another curvy bombshell sashaying down the hallway. She hadn't seen Rick anywhere near her, but the woman had been coming from the direction of his apartment. So many women. So many coincidences.

It was time to face facts and move on. Rick was like smooth, dark chocolate that cost way too much. She'd only had the one taste, so maybe in time she'd be able to forget how incredible he was.

Oh, who was she kidding? Forgetting Rick was going to be the hardest thing she'd ever done. She doubted she was up to the challenge.

As Haley slumped in her chair, she listened to Jen impart more blunt wisdom, her voice muffled behind stacks of boxes and the roar of the furnace. "Based on experiences with three good-looking jerks, you decide you're only going to date men who bore you and leave you cold. Then, a nice guy moves in next door, a *hunk* who makes you laugh and takes care of your dog. He finds you attractive, wants to date you, and you drop him in favor of his schmuck of a cousin. All in the name of some twisted scheme pitting fairy tale frogs against princes." Jen shook her head, her bafflement plain. "And now, finally, you sleep with Rick...and then dump him again because he was *good* at it?"

"No, not because he was good at it. I mean, he *was* good at it, don't get me wrong, but he's, oh, God, so *experienced*. Why would he want me? It doesn't matter.

I'm sure he's already forgotten me and found someone with a bigger bustline."

After a silent moment, Jen responded, her voice firm with conviction. "You're certifiable. I wash my hands of you."

Groaning at the possibility that she'd managed to disgust even Jen with her stupidity, Haley turned to tally the cash register. Seeking escape, Haley spent the rest of the morning rearranging displays, dusting every flat surface she could find and helping customers.

As noon approached, the store grew busy with the usual traffic of lunchtime shoppers and mothers stopping off after their department store excursions. She'd overheard more than one mom refer to the store as a reward for a child's cooperation. That did wring a smile from her. She liked the idea of her store being a reward. Her love life might be a mess, but business was booming.

"Haley! Hello, darling. I was afraid we'd missed you."

Haley looked up in surprised pleasure at the sound of her mother's voice. When she caught sight of Clara—and her companion—Haley groaned inwardly.

Smiling, Clara wove a slender arm through the elbow of the handsome man at her side. The presence of these two beautiful people basically dominated her little toy shop. The mothers were pointing and whispering, and a duo of toddlers stopped destroying a train set display in order to stare. The couple walked up to the counter, where Haley was restocking bags.

"Look, Mom, I hate to be rude, but—"

"Then don't be." She frowned. "Honey, you look pale. Are you all right?"

Haley shifted uncomfortably. "Sure. Just a headache."

The older woman nodded. "I suppose you skipped breakfast again." She waved away Haley's protests. "Don't worry. We can fix that easily enough. Just come along and we'll take you to lunch."

Not budging yet, Haley glanced warily from her mother to the man standing next to her.

"You remember Adam? Adam Harding?" Clara prompted.

"Of course." She nodded and forced a smile. "Hello, Adam." Another setup. So much for butting out of her love life, Haley thought with an inward sigh. Out of habit, she silently chanted herself to patience. *She meant well, she meant well, she meant well....*

"It's good to see you again, Haley. Your mother raves about you."

"I—thanks."

"So, shall we go to lunch?" her mother prompted her.

"Well, I really hate to leave Jen alone when we're this busy." She raised a questioning eyebrow at Jen, who just rolled her eyes and waved her out the door. No doubt Haley's hyperactive saleswoman routine was driving her partner bonkers. A break would be good. "Okay, let's go."

They walked to the soup-and-sandwich place across the street and ordered. Now, seated and nursing a root beer, Haley gazed curiously at the two people across from her. Her mother hadn't stopped smiling since Haley had seen her at the toy shop. But it looked like that smile was trembling around the edges. Haley frowned in concern.

"What's up, Mom?"

Clara exchanged glances with Adam, who smiled back at her before turning back to Haley. "Your mother and I are dating. She's been afraid to tell you."

Blindsided, Haley stared. She glanced back and forth between the couple. And they were a couple. It made sense now. First, there had been that strange conversation with her mother over frozen custard, and then this odd nervousness. It all made scary sense.

"You're dating. Like friends, right?" Haley didn't believe the words even as she spoke them.

"I told you she was naive." Clara glanced fondly at Adam, but her face was tense. She turned back to her daughter. "No. We're dating like a man and a woman." Her eyes narrowed sternly. "And if you dare say 'oh, yuck,'" she copied the words crisply. "I swear I'll take you over my knee here and now."

Haley nodded, trying to rally herself. "So you're *dating* dating." The nod curved into a shaking of her head, a complete rejection of the idea. "But—Adam, how old are you anyway?"

"Haley!" Clara's voice was shocked.

Haley sat back, arms outstretched. "Hey, wouldn't *you* wonder, Mom? You originally planned to set him up with *me*—your daughter. Now you're dating him yourself?"

"I didn't steal him from you. You told me in no uncertain terms to butt out of your social life, so I did. Are you attempting to butt into *my* social life now?"

"Well, it looks like somebody needs to."

"Ladies, please. Look, I don't want to get between you, but can I have my say, too?" Adam smiled uneasily.

Haley sighed. "Of course."

"I'm thirty-seven, Haley. About thirteen years younger than your mother."

"That makes her old enough to be *your* mother."

Clara stared down her nose at her daughter. "Just barely."

Haley rolled her eyes.

Adam smiled at them. "I understand your concern, Haley, but I have to wonder. Have you ever really looked at your mother? Seen more in her than her relationship to you? She's a beautiful woman. She's charming. She's smart. Witty. I enjoy her company very much and I find her incredibly attractive. So we're dating. It's as simple as that."

Haley glanced back and forth. "Oh, yu—"

"Haley Marie Watson! Say it and you'll pay for it."

Haley raised an eyebrow at a laughing Adam. "She sounds like a mother to me."

He cocked his head at her. "Yes, but I think you'll be looking at her a little differently if you let yourself."

Haley shifted uneasily, nibbling at her sandwich and glancing covertly at her mother. Clara looked flushed, angry and embarrassed.

Ashamed, Haley set down her sandwich. "I'm sorry, Mom. I was out of line. I guess I'm not used to the idea of you actually dating yet, and now, well, *this*."

Clara sighed, tried a smile. "I know, and believe it or not, I do understand. But...has it occurred to you that you sometimes...*categorize* people? I'm old, he's young. Nothing's as simple as that, Haley. You need to look deeper."

Haley studied her thoughtfully, her heart leaden. "I'm not sure I see clearly when I look deeper."

Clara smiled with the confident understanding of a mother discussing her daughter's foibles. "Sure, you do. You just don't trust what you see. You try to rationalize it, categorize it, then *tell* yourself what you see. Go with that first, deeper instinct, not the rest. Your heart will show you the truth if you let it."

Long after she'd said her farewells to her mom and Adam and returned to the toy shop to relieve Jen, Haley continued to ponder her mother's unexpected news and even more surprising advice. Alone now in the shop, Haley could admit, privately, to an aching loneliness and an envy for some small part of what her mother had discovered.

Was her mother right after all? Could she trust her judgment where Rick was concerned? She wanted to believe he cared about her, wanted it so bad it hurt.

All day, she'd been reliving the tenderness of his lovemaking, the way he'd cherished her, played with her, and simply understood her on some primitive level. And then there had been that one moment when he'd met her eyes, reached out for her before she'd frozen him out and slammed the door behind him. The connection then had been almost stronger than the physical love they'd shared.

And it had been love, at least on her end. Was it possible that he felt the same way? Frowning and setting her jaw with new determination, Haley decided it was time to stop whining and find out where she stood. Murmuring a quick excuse to Jen, she left to find Rick.

10

"GREG. HI." HALEY EYED HIM with absent curiosity as she dug for her keys. Greg was sitting on the floor outside her apartment and looked like he'd been there for a while.

Clambering to his feet, he offered her a sheepish grin. "I forgot my key and I don't think Rick's coming home for a few hours yet. He's working on a new project. So I was hoping I could camp out on your couch until he gets back. Is that okay?"

Haley forced a smile. After going to the bike shop and finding Rick not there, she'd returned home with the intent of freshening up and cornering him in his apartment. It looked now like she must have just missed him somehow. Damn it. Well, he had to come home sometime, and she'd be waiting for him.

Meanwhile, it looked like she had a guest and they might as well wait together. "Sure, Greg. Come on in." She unlocked the door and led the way inside, dumping keys and purse on a small table.

Sherlock whined his usual welcome from behind a gate at the top of the stairs. As she glanced up at the dog, the smell of a ripe trashcan drifted her way. She wrinkled her nose. Overripe bananas sitting in plastic all day. Yuck.

When the dog saw Greg entering the apartment behind Haley, whining graduated to furious barking. She glanced distractedly over her shoulder at her visitor. "Have a seat while I take the dog out."

Eyeing Sherlock uneasily, Greg dropped onto the couch.

Thinking to save herself a trip, Haley hooked the leash to Sherlock's collar with one hand, plucking up the aromatic trash bag with the other. Woman, trash bag and dog successfully cleared the door, navigated the stairs, then met with disaster in the face of temptation.

The teasing white Persian flitted before them, and Haley could swear she saw the cat toss them a taunting glance over its shoulder. Sherlock lunged after it. Stumbling under the weight of her rapidly growing pet, Haley slammed into the side of the banister, smashing the trash bag against her new blouse.

"Sherlock, stop! Heel! Treat-treat?" The last, desperate plea had Sherlock halting in his tracks and tossing an eager, questioning glance over his shoulder.

Thinking hostile thoughts but keeping her smile firmly in place, Haley murmured sweet nothings to her dog about treat-treats and good boys and teasing little kitty-cats. Keeping up the patter, she managed to dump her trash in an empty can, let the dog do his business and coax Sherlock back up the stairs without further mishap.

Once inside, with Sherlock gnawing on a dog biscuit upstairs, Haley turned her attention to her guest. He was staring. His smile was polite, but his eyes kept glazing over as he stared at her blouse. Thinking the worst, Haley glanced down. She was relieved to see no popped buttons. There was, however, what appeared to be a nasty ketchup stain smeared from breast to breast. Wincing, she remembered the feel of the trash bag smashed between her and the banister. She must have punctured it. Typical.

"Just another doggy adventure," Haley explained, sighing. "Sherlock and I are still settling in." She dabbed at the stain with a wet towel, but it didn't budge. Ruined. She gave up.

Greg nodded. "Rick mentioned that he was helping you train your dog. He's great with animals."

"Yes, he is. In fact, this is the time he usually comes over to train Sherlock." She glanced up, striving for a casual expression. "You said he's working right now?"

"Yeah. Hey, but listen, if Rick said he'd help you with the dog, you can bet he'll be over later to do just that. He's a stand-up kind of guy."

"You really think so?" She flinched at the naked questioning in her own voice.

Greg studied her shrewdly. A rueful grin twisted his lips. "Oh, man. You *really* like him, don't you." It was a statement, not a question.

"Now that would be a stupid move, wouldn't it." She shied away from his gaze, frowning. "The man has so many women fighting for his attention, I'd just be one in a crowd." Stung, she let her pride take over. "The last thing I need in my life is another womanizer, anyway."

Greg laughed. "You've got to be kidding. Womanizer? *Rick?* Not likely. The guy hasn't dated in months."

"Pull the other one."

"No, really. He's been living like a monk. Hell, his mom sends me out here every once in a while because she's afraid he's gay."

"You're kidding." Haley sent him a deadpan expression.

Greg had the grace to blush. "So I'm exaggerating a little. She sends me out here because I need a job and because she *wonders* about his social life. Especially since that stupid talk show—"

"I know all about the talk show and how he's been harassed ever since. But I've seen him with a lot of women. They can't *all* be stalkers. Good grief, just this morning, I ran into another one in the hall outside Rick's door."

After a moment of frowning thought, Greg's eyes brightened and he grinned. Hugely. "Long, black hair, big blue eyes, a chest out to—" He held cupped hands several inches away from his scrawny rib cage.

Haley nodded, annoyed by the enthusiasm of his description.

"That must have been Monika. She was *my* date last night, and, um. Well." He exhaled noisily, his grin boyishly proud as he left the rest to her imagination.

"She was *your* date last night?" Haley glared. "So *she* was the reason you called the other day to break *our* date?"

"Yeah." He turned red, seemed at a loss for words.

Greg was never at a loss for words. Haley frowned. "You're not by any chance covering up for your cousin, are you? Was the beautiful Monika *Rick's* date, not yours?"

"No! Really. Rick's not dating anybody that I know

of. He's so nuts about you, he can barely think straight."

Haley ignored the leap of her heart at Greg's emphatic words. Still, she squashed the hope. "Right. If he's so nuts about me, why did he throw me together with *you?*"

"Okay, so he engineered that first date between you and me. But it's not what you think."

"It looks pretty straightforward to me. He set us up. Period." Folding her arms, she shook her head and used sarcasm to cover the hurt. "Come on, Greg. He's so 'crazy' about me he set me up with another guy?"

Greg sat forward, his eyes intense. "Exactly. That's *exactly* why he set us up. He's nuts about you and he's desperate because you won't even consider dating him. Something about frogs and geeks?" He shook his head, waving a hand obliquely.

Haley felt her cheeks burn with humiliation and the beginnings of temper. "He told you about all that?"

"Well, I am his cousin. We talk."

"Right. Tell me what else you know." Her voice was low and threatening.

Like a small animal cornered and suddenly made aware of incipient danger, Greg blinked cautiously behind the thick lenses of his glasses. "Look, I'm explaining this pretty badly. How about I let Rick tell you—"

"You started this. Finish your story." She smiled grimly. "Then I'll talk to Rick."

"Look, he didn't mean to hurt you. He just wasn't getting anywhere with you. So he needed me to teach you—"

"*Teach* me?" She prompted him, a horrible suspicion forming. "A 'lesson' maybe?"

At her dangerous tone, Greg paused before proceeding more cautiously. "He thought, after a few dates with me, you'd figure out that ugly glasses don't say anything about a guy. Except that he has bad vision."

"And how would I figure that out?" Her eyes narrowed in comprehension. "That first evening, all the stupid innuendo, the cheap lines. It was all an act. You *wanted* me to think you were a jerk."

He smiled crookedly. "Well, maybe I cranked it up a little. The whole point is, whatever I look like, I'm *not* the steady, reliable guy you seem to be looking for. Rick just wanted you to see that."

She forced a laugh. "I bet it ticked him off when I decided you were more misguided than offensive."

Greg shrugged, but nodded.

"So it was all planned. Between the two of you."

"I—yes."

"To teach me a lesson."

"Well...yeah." Shrugging helplessly, Greg seemed to have run out of words.

Haley felt a lump forming in her throat. This was— She'd never suspected Rick would go this far. She swallowed heavily. "He planned all of this out of revenge. Just because he didn't like my reasons for not dating him."

"No!" Greg's voice rose in panic as he launched off the couch. The words came out in a rush. "I mean, maybe a little out of revenge, but not really against you." He began to pace, gesturing with his hands for emphasis. "You need to understand some things about

Rick. He's, well, socially awkward. Really, really good with computers, good with bikes, good with business. Just bad with people."

She snorted her disbelief, fighting desperately to hold the tears back.

"No, seriously." He nudged his glasses up the bridge of his nose before continuing to pace, more slowly as he phrased his thoughts more carefully. "It's only since Computer Nation took hold and started doing so well, that he started changing his image. He learned to be easier around people, took up biking to keep in shape and started wearing contact lenses."

She watched him, confused. "Back up. What does a computer store have to do with Rick's image?"

Greg halted a good distance away and turned to face her with a cautious look in his eyes. He exhaled heavily.

Haley tensed.

"Rick owns the place. The chain, actually. He's loaded. The bike store's more of a hobby." Greg paused to let this sink in before continuing.

"He's always been used to going his own way, but then that talk show aired, and—" he shrugged "—he's been having trouble since then with women. They ignored him before all this and now he can't keep them away. The smell of money, I guess."

Haley took a deep breath, then another, but the urge to kill was still strong. "Let me get this straight. Rick objected to my trying to find a decent husband because he felt it belittled him in some way? So he sicced you on me to teach me a lesson?" She paused, her sarcasm blatant now. "And he did all of this because he's desperately in love with me. Right?"

He thought for a moment before nodding carefully. "That's not quite the way I'd put it, but yeah, that about covers it."

"Got it. Lock up before you leave. I have some errands to run."

"Huh?" He swung around, startled. "Wait, Haley, don't you think you ought to—" she slammed the door behind her, never hearing him finish "—change your shirt?"

OH, THE NERVE OF THAT self-righteous, manipulative, conceited jerk. To think she'd believed herself in love with him.

So he thought to teach her a lesson, did he? He actually concocted this elaborate scheme just to show her how wrong she was in her thinking. If she was deceived and humiliated in the process, well, so much the better. She could only suppose that he intended the humbled, infinitely smarter Haley Watson to run screaming from the offensive geek and straight into his macho arms, begging for a turn in his bed. At which point, he'd tell her thanks, but no thanks. Class dismissed.

Ha. Not in this lifetime.

Slamming her car door shut, Haley fumed all the way into the store, down an aisle, eyes flicking this way and that in search of walking slime. It turned out the slime wasn't walking but seated contentedly behind his desk. She zeroed in.

STARING AT THE COMPUTER and seeing only Haley's face on the screen, Rick shook himself back to reality. It was useless. He couldn't concentrate. All he could think about was what had happened at Haley's apartment right before everything fell apart.

First, there was the mind-blowing sex on the couch. No, not sex. Lovemaking. For the first time in his life he had actually *made love* to a woman, because he did love her. That tiny, hot little body, a livewire of energy. He loved her quirky sense of humor, the softness in her eyes, her exuberance when she stopped driving him wild to look at him and touch his face. He remembered that look so clearly, as well as the passion and hurt in her eyes as he walked out her door. She loved him. She had to.

And now it was time to stop playing games and start acting like an adult. He was going to admit everything to her about that stupid plan he and Greg had invented. He'd let her kick and scream and dole out whatever punishment she thought he deserved. Then he would tell her that he loved her and wanted her more than anything or anyone in his life.

With an exasperated series of mouse clicks, he turned off the computer and rose from his chair. As he turned to open the glass door of his office, it slammed open, catching him smartly across the face. He stumbled backward.

"You jerk. You overbearing, arrogant, conceited, know-it-all, self-righteous *jerk.*" Haley's brown eyes glittered with rage.

His throbbing nose forgotten, Rick stared down at her in shock. "Haley—"

"So you wanted to teach me a lesson, huh? Sic your cousin on me just to prove a point? I guess I was supposed to learn he was smart but as dependable as a flea, then come running to you, my deceiving prince?"

Rick felt his stomach drop. "It wasn't like that. I swear it wasn't like that. It's just that you had this image of the perfect guy for you, and I didn't fit it. You wouldn't even consider me."

"And you thought manipulating me would convince me to give you a chance?"

He felt his own temper rise. "I wasn't manipulating you any more than you were manipulating all those poor schmucks you tried to pick up. Guys like Tim and Jared didn't stand a chance against those drippy brown eyes you were giving them. And you didn't even like either one of them. You were just playing with their heads for your own selfish reasons."

Her face went still, her brown eyes huge. "You accuse me of playing games with men's minds, and then you go and do the same thing to me. Just to teach me a lesson. Don't you see something wrong with that? Do you think that's the way to prove to me that you have honest feelings for me?"

"No, but—"

She waved him to silence. "My methods might have been a little unorthodox, but I didn't intend to hurt anyone. I just wanted to find a man I could trust with my future. What's so wrong with that?" Her eyes were steady on his, the hurt plain for him to see.

Rick opened his mouth to protest, feeling his own future crumble around him. After a silent moment, he closed it again, his heart heavy. She was right. He hadn't meant to hurt her, but he'd been pretty arrogant in assuming he had the right to teach her a lesson. "I'm sorry."

She glared at him, the pain evident behind her anger. "You know, Greg tried to defend this scheme of yours. He told me you used to be what everyone considered a geek. One who didn't have a clue how to deal with people, much less manipulate them. I say it's a shame you changed so much."

Rick stared, speechless, as she turned sharply and walked away.

She stalked through the store, the satisfaction of having the last word dissipating so fast it left her dizzy and sick. She wanted nothing more than to get out of this store and find someplace private to vomit in peace.

Blindly, she hurried through the aisles, turned a corner and collided. As she did so, she felt the heel on her shoe breaking off. Just wonderful. Busted her favorite shoes, stained her silk blouse and discovered she was the world's biggest fool. A great day all around.

"Haley?" After steadying her and setting her back on her feet, Tim adjusted his glasses and peered down at her.

Studying his face, Haley recognized the salesclerk who had taken her on her first, unremarkable geek date. Boring but genuine. Undoubtedly decent. Didn't do a thing for her. Jen was right. She was most definitely certifiable. "Hi, Tim." She fidgeted, looking over his shoulder and gauging the distance between her and the door.

"Are you okay?" He frowned at her, obviously reading some of her distress. His gaze lowered to the stain on her blouse, there pausing to stare in wide-eyed concern. "You're bleeding." He stepped forward, hand outstretched.

She dodged it. "Not blood. Ketchup. Look, I have to go, okay?" She gave him a wobbly smile and made another try for the door, her gait an uneven, up-down rhythm to accommodate the broken shoe.

As she paused to let a family pass, she heard whispers coming from behind her.

"Tim, who was that?" The voice was female and not sufficiently muffled.

"Just a girl I went out with once."

"Where did you ever find her?" she asked in a giggling undertone.

"Aw, come on, Missy. Give her a break. She's nice. Just a little weird. Kind of a geek, really."

Haley froze. After a moment of complete silence, she continued walking, her hobbling stride careful, her face on fire.

WATCHING HALEY'S APARTMENT door slam in his face for the third time just that day, Rick sighed and slumped defeatedly. He should have chased the stubborn woman down before she left his store, and he would have if he hadn't stumbled over his own guilt. Now he was reduced to wangling moments of Haley's time so he could beg her to understand and give him what? A third chance? Fourth? Fifth?

But what else could a guy do when he'd screwed up this badly? He couldn't give up. It was Haley or no one for him. All he could do was wait her out and keep trying. He'd have to wear her down all over again, just

She glanced down at the paisley tie. The shocking fuschia and purple print was rendered even more offensive by the baby blue shade of his elastic suspenders. She felt near-hysterical tremors building deep inside. The crazy intensity grew until she shook with it, finally surrendering to the joyous release of mingled laughter and tears.

Looking up at him through a blurred haze and a huge smile, she carefully lifted the eyeglasses from his face and found those blazingly blue eyes that haunted her every night in her dreams. For the past week, she'd pictured those eyes everywhere, in every emotional state from laughter to anger to desire. Now, she saw love in them.

With a broken laugh, she shook her head. "You don't have to change. Except maybe out of this getup. You made your point. And, as much as I hate to inflate your ego, I've learned my lesson, too. You're not a geek, and you're not a jerk. You're so much more than that. You're everything I've ever wanted in a man. Heaven help me, but I love you, Rick Samuels."

As his mouth closed possessively over hers, she vaguely registered some light applause and the deafening sounds of juvenile disgust coming from behind her. Ignoring all of it, Haley gave herself up to his kiss. She smiled against his lips as she came to a new realization.

It had been a long time in coming, but maybe, just maybe, she'd found her very own frog.

__Epilogue__

CLARA WATSON SMILED SWEETLY from the TV screen. "I have a special postscript to add to today's Show Me Show. As you know, whenever we have new information on past stories, we like to share with our viewers."

Clara's lashes lowered and she appeared amazingly feline. "Several weeks ago, we aired a show featuring the ten most eligible bachelors in St. Louis." Her expression grew crafty.

"What the?" Rick sat up in bed and reached for the remote.

"I knew a TV in the bedroom was a bad thing." Haley opened her eyes reluctantly. "I can't believe I'm sharing my post-coital bliss with my mother."

"Shh." Rick's eyes were rapt on the TV as he used the remote to rewind the tape.

Haley had taken to taping her mother's programs ever since the surprise bachelor show. They usually watched the tape after dinner but had gotten blissfully sidetracked tonight with a rousing new game Rick had entitled "Connect the Freckles." She was pretty certain he'd connected every last one of them.

Groaning now at the discordant concept of her mother's voice chirping into their bedroom, Haley propped an elbow behind her so she could focus on the screen.

like he had the first time. Only, this time, he'd have to do it honestly. No more secrets, no more manipulations.

"Hi, Mr. Samuels," a little voice chirped from behind him.

"Hmm? Oh, hi, Christopher. How's it going, buddy?" Rick tried to smile. Christopher was a great kid. Exceptionally bright. Plus, they shared a common obsession for the latest computer games.

"Okay." Christopher smiled, his cheeks flushing. "Tommy Corrington invited me to his birthday party. All the kids are going."

Rick's smile grew more genuine. "That's great, Chris."

"Yeah." His smile faded and he glanced at the closed apartment door. "How come Aunt Haley slammed the door like that? Doesn't she like you anymore?"

Rick leaned against the wall. "You could say that. I did something really stupid. Something I shouldn't have done. Now she won't even talk to me."

Christopher widened his eyes with childlike drama. "It must have been really bad. Haley likes everybody."

"Yeah, she does, doesn't she? I didn't know it at first, but I do now." He looked down at Christopher. "Got any great ideas for making her like me again?"

Christopher squinched up his eyes in thought. After a moment, his face brightened. "I know. You could borrow my joke book. She says people forget I'm short when they're laughing. They just think I'm funny and then they like me. Maybe she'll forget you made her mad if she's laughing at your jokes."

Rick grinned. "Think so?"

"Sure. Wanna borrow it?"

Rick ruffled the boy's hair. "I'm not sure it would work with her. She's pretty mad at me. Thanks for the hint, though."

"Sure."

A feminine voice called from down the hallway. "Christopher. Time for dinner."

Christopher grimaced. "I gotta go. Mom doesn't like it if I'm late for dinner."

"Better not keep her waiting, then." Rick smiled.

"Right. I hope you can make Aunt Haley like you again."

"Me, too." He watched the little boy race down the hallway and disappear inside an apartment.

He was glad Christopher had found his niche in school. Haley's joke book had been an impressive idea. Everyone did indeed like to laugh, and a good comedian could always make friends. Too bad Christopher's idea wouldn't work for him, too.

Or would it?

"HALEY, WHY DON'T YOU GO on home. I can handle things here."

Pausing to adjust her grip on a box she was carrying out to the sales floor, Haley tossed an incredulous look at her partner. The signs she and Jen had set out on the sidewalk in front of the toy store had drawn the crowd of their dreams. In short, they were swamped. "If you think I'm leaving you alone in the middle of all this, you're nuts. I'll be fine. I can barely think right now, which is exactly what I need."

Jen eyed her worriedly, then turned back to the line

of customers at the cash register. Haley continued out to the sales floor with the last box of Beanie Babies they had in stock. She just set it on the floor and stood back while the kids fell on it like starving animals over a fresh kill. Amid the squeals and giggles, Haley was surprised to find herself giggling right along with the squirmy mass of pint-sized excitement.

One particularly enterprising toddler literally climbed over the huddled children and into the box. To his mother's halfhearted protests, he started tossing the animal-shaped beanbags over his shoulder in an effort to find something he called Gumbie Grilla.

As Haley approached, intending to intervene tactfully, she heard the distinctive crack of plush-covered beans hitting glass. She looked over her shoulder and directly into a familiar, if slightly disjointed gaze. Her eyes widened in shock.

Behind a set of clunky-framed eyeglass lenses was a pair of sexy blue eyes no optometry could disguise. True, whatever he'd used to slick back his hair had darkened the golden strands to a more burnished hue, but even that just looked exotic to her.

Her lips started to quiver as she let her gaze drift past what looked to be a Gumbie Grilla now perched on his shoulder. A wrinkled white shirt and stained paisley tie topped off navy polyester pants pulled up to *here* and held in place by a pair of powder blue suspenders. His pants legs ended at the anklebones, revealing his socks and scuffed saddle shoes. Where in the world had he found *saddle shoes?* she wondered distractedly.

Shifting nervously—painfully?—in those ugly shoes,

Rick smiled his lopsided grin. It wasn't a practiced expression, but more of a hopeful one that expected to be crushed at any moment. "I, um, heard you had a sale on Beanie Babies?"

She choked back a surprised laugh before stepping aside and gesturing to the nearly empty box behind her. The crowd had thinned and reorganized into a long line at the cash register. The satisfying *cha-ching* sound repeating itself over and over again did her entrepreneur's heart good. Too bad her heart needed more than sales to keep it happy. She turned back to find Rick standing directly in front of her.

Meeting his gaze, she felt anew the humiliation and anger of these past few days. Her throat tightened. She swallowed heavily, spoke low. "What do you want?"

"You." He reached up to touch her cheek with a gentle finger.

Feeling herself weaken, she pulled back and shifted her gaze from the hypnotic blue that sapped her will so dangerously.

He dropped his hand but held his ground. She watched the paisley tie rise and lower with his breathing. It seemed erratic. A lot like hers.

"Haley, what I want is to tell you I'm sorry. You were right. I acted like the same conceited, insensitive jerks you've been trying to avoid. If I could take away the hurt I caused you, I would. But I can't." He paused. "So, I took some advice from a mutual friend and decided to try to make you smile instead."

Still avoiding his eyes, she watched his lips curve slightly.

"As you can see, I'm a changed man now." Plucking